NELLE HERAN &
C.K. EASTLAND

Cover art: Covers in Color, coversincolor.com
Edited by: Sunwalker Press; Meg DesCamp

ISBN: 978-1-947033-44-3

First edition
August 2022

Contact information:
ejr@ejrussell.com
ck@ckeastland.com

MIXED MEDIA

Crafty Sleuth

NELLE HERAN &
C.K. EASTLAND

CHAPTER ONE

"LaTashia Danielle Fredericka Van Buren." My bestie, PJ, studied me from the sidewalk in front of the Airship Ambassador Tearoom and Apothecary in his knee-length army surplus overcoat and black skinny jeans, swinging a galvanized metal bucket in his hand. "I know that look. You're thinking about *crafting*, aren't you?"

I held open the plate glass door that led to the tearoom's gift shop and gestured for him to come inside. "Of course I'm thinking about crafting. You're delivering the supplies for the mosaic project yourself."

He glanced down at the bucket with its load of newly cleaned pennies. "A point. But—"

The door to the bar that shared the tearoom's building burst open and a man wearing jeans, a denim jacket, and an orange hard hat stormed onto the sidewalk. The scowl on his face was darker than the Oregon clouds, and he didn't change his trajectory at all to avoid PJ. He caromed into PJ, not even pausing to apologize, and strode off down the street.

PJ stumbled, and in the struggle to regain his balance, he lost his grip on the bucket. It fell at his feet, scattering pennies across the sidewalk like bright copper confetti. He propped his fists on his hips. "Rude!" He turned to me and pointed at the man's retreating back. "And did you *see* the size of the bit on that drill he was carrying? I could have been *impaled*."

I stepped out of the tearoom, the door swinging closed behind me with a tinkle of its vintage bell. "Are you okay?"

To many, PJ and I made an odd pair. Me, a six-foot-and-a-hair plus-sized Black woman, and PJ, a bespectacled hipster white guy several inches shorter—although PJ never copped to *short, small,* or *average.* "I'm medium," he was fond of saying. But we shared a similar love of fashion, flair, and fun, and had become besties almost since the first moment we'd met during our orientation at our mutual employer. Although I could never entice him to explore any of my crafting projects, he was always there to support me in whatever way I needed. We had each other's backs, and always would.

I started to crouch down to help him gather the pennies, but he waved me away. "I'm fine, but if I recall this project, you and Margaret have been kneeling on the floor for *hours* already. I've got this." He scrunched his face as he picked up a penny. "Although I'll need to clean these *again.* Honestly, the Beaverton City Council should do a better job of keeping their sidewalks swept."

I couldn't deny that my knees were feeling the effect of a morning spent helping my friend Margaret Needham, the tearoom's co-owner, piece a steampunk airship mosaic on the floor of the unfinished restroom. "If you're sure?"

"Positive." He flapped his hands again. "Now shoo. Just leave the door on the latch for me and I'll join you after I've gathered the slightly grimy largesse. Besides"—he glanced up at the clouds—"it's about to rain and your Afro puff is much too fabulous today to risk a wetting."

I tucked an errant curl behind my ear, blew him a kiss, and stepped back into the gift shop. Since the tearoom was closed today, as it was every Monday and Tuesday, the space was dim, lit only by daylight through the plate-glass windows. The display cases next to the register held designer candies and were topped by jewelry carousels. Whitewashed vintage hutches and Victorian side tables were decked with artisan candles, tins of the Airship Ambassador's signature tea blends, and specialty art pieces—many made by me. As I walked through, I noted some of the merchandise was getting sparse. My Alice in Wonderland cards were running low, as were the clockwork butterfly earrings, and those partly empty shelves just begged for some new, seasonally inspired artwork. With Halloween coming up next month, it was a perfect time to add some spooky-themed goodies to the gift shop. I pictured them in my mind. Nothing huge—small, mixed media shadowboxes with a gothic/steampunk flair and a Disney Haunted-Mansionish vibe. I made a mental note to mention it to Margaret.

When I stepped through the curtains that masked the gift shop from the dining room, I had to stop and take a breath, contentment stealing over me as it did with every visit. I adored the steampunk aesthetic. Antiques mingled with two- and four-top tables covered with white linen and preset with mismatched china for the Airship Ambassador's version of high tea. A classic dirigible model ran the length of the ceiling above the long family-serve table in front of the large fireplace. Colored lights inside the dirigible's fabric gave the entire area a warm, cozy glow. Birdcages and bowler hats covered faux-vintage Tesla bulb fixtures hung from the high tin-covered ceilings. On the wall opposite the high oak counter separating the dining room from the prep area and kitchen hung a portrait of the Airship Ambassador himself in an ornate antique gilded frame. His eyes seemed to follow you no matter where you stood. Yes, this tearoom vied with Central Paper and Supply as my all-time favorite place.

I walked toward the restrooms, my black and white Chucks squeaking along the sealed concrete floor. When I peeked through the door at the end of the hall, Margaret was still kneeling where I'd left her, positioning two pennies on the airship's gondola, her silver-shot brown hair escaping from her messy bun.

"PJ's here with more pennies," I said.

"Good, because those are the last of my current supply." She sat back on her haunches, studying the three-quarters-finished mosaic with her head tilted to one side. "I was a little unsure if the dirigible proportions were right for the size of the room, but I think it works, don't you?"

"It's brilliant. It's a great companion piece to the deep-sea motif in the other restroom."

Her wide brow pleated in a frown. "I just wish we hadn't needed to carve out floor space for this one."

"Considering how much tea your customers consume, it's probably a good thing."

"Yes, but we were booked solid for weeks in advance with the old layout, and we lost four tables with this build-out. We wouldn't have started this renovation if the owner of the Rip Snorter next door hadn't told us he was retiring. Hank and I were so excited. We had offers on the table to Jeffrey Tillman, our landlord, one to lease the Rip Snorter space and one to buy the whole building outright. We could have murdered the man when we found out he was bringing in another bar without bothering to even discuss it with us."

I shivered a little at her words. I'd had way too much experience with murder last summer to be comfortable with tossing the word around casually. "Have you ever thought about branching out to another location? Someplace with more room?" Angry raised voices filtered in from next door, and I winced. "Or quieter neighbors? Wow, these walls have lousy soundproofing."

"Trust me, we're aware." Margaret braced one hand against the wall and rose to her feet. "We thought about extending our hours, maybe adding a cocktail service, but the sound of drunk people whooping over a mechanical bull or wailing along to country-western karaoke doesn't exactly fit with our ambience."

"No. It really doesn't."

"I come bearing pennies," PJ proclaimed from the doorway, brandishing his bucket, "broken but unbowed. Margaret, my love, you're looking radiant as usual."

"Broken?" I frowned at him worriedly. "Did that rude construction guy come back?"

"No. Although an extremely snitty fellow in a truly unfortunate green tweed suit, waving his clipboard like Excalibur, chased after him and nearly upset the pennies *again*. However, I prevailed, as you see, despite the looming zombie apocalypse." He bowed.

Have I mentioned that PJ can be a tad dramatic? But his words sparked an idea. "Speaking of zombie apocalypses..." I said.

Margaret's eyebrows rose as she edged around the mosaic to join us at the door. "Are there more than one?"

PJ kissed her cheek. "There are as many as the market will bear, my darling. Simply say the word, and you and Hank can join Tash and me in a bingefest across *all* the streaming platforms."

Muffled voices and high-pitched yells bled through from the bar. Margaret jerked her thumb toward it. "No, thanks. If I'm in the mood for apocalyptic mayhem, all I have to do is—"

The wall shook under a deafening *bang*, followed by a thundering *crash*.

PJ fumbled the bucket, but caught it at the last minute. "Was that from your kitchen?"

Margaret stared at me, wide-eyed. "Hank," she croaked, and pushed past us into the hallway.

CHAPTER TWO

PJ and I rushed after her. Margaret's husband Hank, the tearoom's other co-owner, herniated a few discs during his final tour of duty as a Marine. His back still bothered him, and he often used an ornately carved walking stick to aid his mobility. If he'd lost his balance and fallen…

But when we joined Margaret in the dining room, Hank was calmly emerging from the kitchen's swinging door. He held a laden tea tray in both hands and was limping a little since he'd clearly left his stick behind.

He raised his eyebrows at the three of us, since we were panting and probably looked a little wild-eyed. "Is something wrong?"

"We—we heard a crash," Margaret said. "We thought you might have…" She gulped as she fought back her initial panic.

Hank slid the tray onto the counter so he could give his wife a hug. "That was next door. The contractors working on the bar renovations can't seem to do anything quietly."

She sagged a little in his embrace. "Thank goodness." She stepped back. "Not that they're noisy next door, but that you're all right."

"Never better." He turned to PJ and held out his fist. PJ bumped it, then they tapped both elbows and pretended to throw salt over their left shoulder in the weird greeting they'd developed during our annual trip to Steam Pirates of the Air and Sea Con in Seattle. "Boo-yah!" they chorused.

PJ shed his overcoat and hung it on the bentwood coat rack. He inhaled the steam drifting up from one of the teapots. "Mmmm. Is that what I think it is?"

Hank chuckled. "Of course. Malachi McCormick's Decent Tea. By now, I know better than to serve you anything else."

PJ held his hand over his heart. "You make me sound *inflexible*, my brother."

Hank nudged one of the other pots toward PJ. "So you're willing to try a London Fog or a cinnamon plum tea?"

PJ slapped Hank's hand. "Paws off my Malachi. As if I'd ever betray him for bergamot or chamomile."

Hank smirked at him. "That's what I thought."

"Please," PJ said as he picked up the tray, "I'm simply very faithful to those I love." He marched over to the table by the window. "And I'm absolutely devoted to my Malachi." He lifted the four teapots off the tray one at a time and arranged one in front of each place. "Well? Are you going to join me or what?"

Hank's booming laugher rolled over us. "Let me get the scones, and I'll be right there."

"I'll get the scones," Margaret said severely. "You get your stick and sit down."

"Yes, dear," Hank said, and winked at us. The two of them disappeared into the kitchen.

When I joined PJ at the table, he pointed at a teapot festooned with fluffy pink peonies. "That's your Russian Trade Route blend. I can tell by the smoky vanilla aroma." After I sat down on the purple velvet upholstered chair opposite him, he leaned forward and whispered, "Have you told them yet?"

"Told us what?" Margaret set two triple-tiered china pastry towers on the table.

"It's not like you to keep secrets from us, Tash." Hank settled into a chair that resembled an overstuffed antique throne, resting his stick against the neighboring table. "I think I'm hurt."

"Hank," Margaret said, fond exasperation lacing her tone. She took a seat next to him. "He doesn't mean it."

"I know. It's nothing dire. The only reason it's a secret is that I'm a little superstitious." I took a deep breath. "I've wanted to take this step for several years now, but inheriting all those craft supplies last summer convinced me that it's time. I've outgrown my apartment." My hands shook a little as I adjusted the cat's-eye sunglasses perched on top of my head. "I've decided to buy a house."

Both of them grinned and Margaret clapped her hands. "That's wonderful, Tash!"

"Absolutely." Hank leaned forward, both hands propped on the head of his stick. "If anyone is responsible enough for home ownership, it's you." He chuckled. "And with your vast circle of acquaintances, you'll have no trouble getting the muscle you need to move. Have you found a real estate agent yet? We used a terrific one when we bought our place. I can give you her card."

I reached over to pat his hand. "Thank you, Mr. Connector. I appreciate the offer, but I'm already working with someone."

"Here we go," PJ muttered into his cup.

I kicked his foot under the table. "Rhonda Robertson."

"Rhonda?" Margaret shared a glance I couldn't interpret with Hank. "Hasn't she been to one of your parties here? The Dickens tea last Christmas, maybe? Or the Mad Tea Party in the spring?"

I nodded. "The Mad Tea Party. She was the one who showed up with a hamper of chamomile tea and a tote bag of Hershey's Kisses because she thought it was an anger intervention."

"I don't like to say anything against one of your friends," Margaret said slowly.

"Oh, don't hold back, Margaret." PJ set his cup on its saucer with a *clink*. "I can't be the only one sounding the danger klaxon."

"Are you sure Rhonda's the right one for the job?" Margaret asked. "I didn't even realize she was an agent."

"She's not," PJ said.

I glared at him. "She's just starting out." I smoothed my napkin over my lap. "I'm actually her first client."

"Tash—" Margaret began.

"Everybody is new at their job *sometime*," I said a little desperately, since I wasn't sure if I was trying to convince them or myself. Goodness knows I hadn't managed to convince PJ yet. "Right out of engineering school, my first boss made me give a very technical presentation to a tough room full of salesmen. My next boss and future mentor were both in that crowd, and he hired me on the strength of that preso, setting me on the path that led to the product management gig I have today. They took a chance on me. I just want to pay it forward."

"That's very commendable and exactly what I'd expect from you." Hank's eyebrows drew together. "But are you positive that it's the best reason to hire a professional who's supposed to help you make one of the biggest investments of your life? You need to be able to depend on her advice."

PJ jabbed the table with one finger. "Exactly!"

I chuckled because PJ and I had replayed this very conversation from the moment I told him I'd be working with Rhonda. "I won't only be relying on her. One of my good friends is married to a home inspector—"

"Another one of your crafting friends?" Margaret asked with a smirk.

"As a matter of fact, no. She's in my writers' group. But she's told me more than once that in a real estate transaction, the only person really working for the buyer is the home inspector. The agents are all getting paid by the seller."

Hank nodded, his frown clearing. "Very true."

"So I'll be able to help Rhonda get her new career off the ground, but I'm also hiring Jim to be my home inspector." I leaned forward and dropped my voice to a stage whisper. "His inspections are *very* thorough. The Realtors in McMinnville refer to him as the Angel of Death because he's killed so many deals."

Margaret hooted a laugh. "He sounds like somebody who needs a steampunk alter ego."

I blinked, struck by the idea. "He'd look like a steampunk Santa. He's got the white beard and the somewhat upholstered middle."

Hank patted his own belly. "I approve of upholstery. It shows an appreciation of the finer things."

Margaret kissed his cheek. "And gives a woman something to hug."

I held up my hand for Margaret to give me a high-five, since my tastes leaned more toward cinnamon roll than protein bar when it came to men, too. My goddess frame deserved a substantial man to cuddle without worrying about snapping him in two or smothering the poor guy with my ample bosom—although I suspected many guys wouldn't mind that particular cause of death.

My last gentleman friend, Bjorn the neo-Viking, was as tall as an old growth tree, ripped to the nines, with a bank account that made most gold diggers swoon. Unfortunately, his ego was proportional to his size, and his penchant for telling lies to compensate for his wandering eye made any future with him impossible. Trust is the foundation of any good relationship, and I found that trust was severely lacking in Bjorn's case.

The sound of the argument next door broke out again, louder this time, but still muffled. Margaret and Hank shared an annoyed glance. "I suppose it's too much to hope that Tillman has insisted the new tenants improve the soundproofing," Hank muttered.

PJ huffed. "You'd think we were in the middle of an episode of *Real Housewives*." He glared over his shoulder as one of the angry voices escalated. "This is ruining the ambience. So inconsiderate. If they're going to argue, the least they could is increase the volume so we can understand what they're saying."

Margaret raised her eyebrows. "You actually want to hear it?"

He winked at her. "Drama is my life's-blood, darling, and my world has been sadly drama-free lately, if you don't count daily clashes with the micromanagers at Jensin Tech." His eyes behind his glasses held the manic gleam that I'd learned to be wary of.

"PJ," I said, lacing my tone with warning, although I doubted it would do any good. "What are you thinking?"

"I intend to go over there and confront the general contractor."

While I knew PJ was brave, he wasn't exactly a strapping specimen, and he was right—the guy who'd run into him on the sidewalk had a really big drill. Plus, construction sites as a whole were chock full of potential weapons—hammers, screwdrivers, box knives, crowbars—any of which could turn deadly, or at least really, really damaging.

"Peej, that's a little risky, don't you think? And we really don't have any business interfering."

He grinned at me. "Calm down, LaTashia. The GC is my cousin. If *I* can't give him grief for all this noise, who can?"

"Do you really think your cousin will thank you for walking in during an argument?"

He stood up. "Trust me. Del is the least argumentative person on the planet. He'll be thrilled for an interruption."

"PJ—" I began, but he was already out of his chair and zipping through the curtain into the gift shop. The front door deadbolt clicked open, and the curtains billowed in the incoming breeze before the door snicked closed. I turned to Margaret and Hank. "I'm sorry. I know you prefer not to let unknown people into the place when you're closed."

"Not random strangers, no," Hank said as he folded his napkin and rose. "But PJ's cousin? That's another story." He smiled down at me. "If he's as entertaining as PJ, we may have to start an open mic night. I'll grab another pot of tea." He collected his stick. "I doubt PJ will share his Malachi, even with a cousin."

Hank ambled off toward the kitchen, stick tapping its familiar rhythm. I could have corrected him. I probably should have. Because if I knew one thing about PJ, it was that once he accepted you into his circle, he'd share anything and everything with you.

Even a pot of his favorite tea.

CHAPTER THREE

The argument next door cut off abruptly. After a few moments, Margaret and I could make out the sound of PJ's voice, rising and falling, followed by laughter.

Margaret shared a grin with me. "Seems like PJ has worked his magic again. I swear, when that man isn't driving you absolutely mad, or making you roll on the floor with laughter, he could charm a rattlesnake."

"Funny," I said, warmth pooling in my middle. "He's said similar things about me. Although I only drive him mad when I'm trying to coerce him into trying a craft."

The curtains billowed again, and the murmur of voices—PJ's light tenor and a deeper baritone rumble—filtered in from the gift shop, followed by the unmistakable solid thunk of the door closing. I smirked at Margaret. Whatever PJ's hapless cousin's opinion of being dragged into a steampunk tea shop might be, PJ had no intention of letting the poor man escape.

PJ emerged from behind the curtain. Well, most of him did, anyway. One hand was still out of sight, no doubt with a death grip on his poor cousin. PJ's smile was so wide it resembled a ventriloquist's dummy and, frankly, was a little creepy. "Hank, Margaret, Tash—may I present my cousin, Del Purdy?"

He yanked once to no apparent effect other than turning his freakish grin into a grimace. But with the second yank—which he braced his feet to deliver two-handed—Del stumbled into the room and smiled sheepishly at us.

Well.

If somebody had asked me to imagine what a cousin of PJ's would look like, I would never have drawn a mental picture of Del Purdy. For one thing, he was tall. Taller than me by at least two or three inches, if I didn't miss my guess. And while PJ was brown-haired, brown-eyed, and artfully scruffed, Del had sandy blond hair, gray eyes, and a full beard. He was wearing a brown canvas Carhartt jacket, a dark green Henley, and jeans that were clearly functional rather than fashionable. A leather tool belt hung around his hips, dipping a little low in front because, like Hank, he had a little upholstery. But if you asked me, it went well with his broad shoulders and clearly powerful frame.

From his expression, though, he was thoroughly mortified by being dragged in to face us all. So I stood up and crossed to him, my hand held out.

"Hello, Del. I'm Tash. It's lovely to meet you."

He glanced down at my hand and then at his own. "I— Sorry, I've been working, so I don't want to, you know, get my grubby all over you."

"There's a restroom down the hall if you'd like to wash up." I gestured at the table, where Hank had also stood up. "We'd love for you to join us for tea if you've got time for a break."

"He does," PJ declared, and all but frog-marched Del down the hall to the finished restroom. He shoved the poor man inside and closed the door, then stood outside with his arms crossed, tapping his foot, as if he was afraid Del would try to make a break for it.

"Are we that scary?" I murmured.

"No!" PJ whispered back. "And that's the point. He moved here two months ago, but he hasn't made the slightest effort to make any new friends." He glanced at the door and his expression softened. "He's a little shy."

"Then why are you forcing him to do this?"

He heaved a dramatic sigh. "Because he's family. And so are you. He needs a circle of fabulous friends, and you're the best people I know."

"All right then. Bring him over to the table when he's done. We'll try not to be too intimidating."

Margaret had already added another chair at the head of the table and Hank had set a fresh pot of tea in front of it. If Del took the seat as expected, he'd be between me and Margaret. Since PJ was on my other side, I could act as a buffer if PJ tried to get a little too forceful in his friending attempts on his cousin's behalf.

When PJ led Del toward us by the elbow, I donned my best welcoming smile. "We're so glad you could join us, Del. Won't you sit down?"

He glanced at PJ, who glared at him. Del didn't seem reluctant to join us so much as uncomfortable. After PJ released him to take his own seat, Del kept his elbows tucked into his sides as though he was afraid he'd send one of Margaret's lovely decorations or vintage teapots crashing to the floor. He started to sit, but his tool belt got caught on the edge of the table, nearly toppling the closest three-tiered pastry tower.

"Sh—" He glanced from me to Margaret. "Shoot. I'm sorry. I just—"

"Take the silly tool belt off, Del," PJ said. "There's no need to look macho in a tearoom, for pity's sake."

Del flushed, his cheeks above his beard turning a rosy pink. "That's not why…" He sighed and unbuckled the belt, but then seemed at a loss about where to set it.

"Don't mind PJ," I said as I stood. "We all know him well enough not to take what he says too seriously."

"So now the truth comes out, eh, LaTashia? You regularly ignore me. Is that what you're saying?"

"No. I'm saying give your cousin a break." I held out my hand to Del again. "If you'll give your tool belt to me, I can put it aside for you so you can enjoy your tea."

"Th-thanks." He handed it over with a shy smile. "Pete's told me about you."

I raised my eyebrows. "'Pete?'"

PJ huffed. "How many times have we discussed this, *Delbert*? It's PJ. You haven't forgotten since we were sixteen, unless you're..." PJ's gaze bounced between me and his cousin, his eyes rounding behind his glasses. "Ooohhh." He waved one hand. "Carry on."

I cast a quizzical glance at PJ before I took Del's tool belt over to the counter. When I set it down, one of the pockets flipped open and a pair of needle-nosed pliers with rainbow rubber grips and jaws the length of my middle finger spilled out. I smiled—I recognized that tool. PJ had given me an identical pair for my birthday the year we met. I tucked them back into the pocket and snapped it closed. When I got back to the table, Margaret was pouring tea into Del's cup.

"So, Del," she said with a smile, "PJ tells us you're new to the area."

He nodded. "That's right. Just moved up from Southern California a couple of months ago." He took a sip of the tea. "Mmmm." He smiled beatifically. "I love tea."

"Also not macho," PJ muttered.

I glared at him. "Why do you say that as though macho were a good thing? You know how I feel about toxic masculinity." I'd gotten more than enough of that from Bjorn, who *still* didn't understand that you couldn't hand-wave lies and emotional unavailability by attempting to camouflage them with expensive gifts.

PJ huffed. "I know, I know. I feel exactly the same." He picked up his cup and put on a decent approximation of an innocent expression. "I'll be good." As hard as that was for me to believe—I knew PJ, after all, and as he said, he lived for drama—based on the rueful smile he gave Del, there was obviously love between them. "Sorry, Del. You know how glad I am to have you around." He brightened. "And look at you, making friends! Our mothers will be *ecstatic*."

Del shifted uncomfortably. "I've just been busy since I got here. Long shifts on the job next door because of problems with some of the local subcontractors." He sighed. "The seller's timeline is pretty short—"

"Seller?" Hank said sharply. "Don't you mean the lessee?"

Del blinked at him. "No. Mr. Tillman is definitely offloading the place, and even in its current state, he managed to find a buyer. He's pushing through the upgrades because they're a condition of the sale."

Margaret set her teacup down with a rattle. The expression on her usually cheerful face was absolutely murderous. "I don't *believe* it. He *promised* us."

"I need to make a call." Hank grabbed his stick and rose from his chair—and if I thought Margaret looked as if she had vengeance on her mind, she had nothing on Hank. He stalked off toward the kitchen where his office was located, and this time, the staccato rap of his stick sounded more like a machine gun.

Del looked from Hank's retreating back to Margaret, who was balling her napkin up as if she wished it were a sensitive part of Jeffrey Tillman's anatomy. "Did I say something wrong?"

"No." Margaret tempered the terse word—slightly—with a tight smile. "It's just that we've wanted to buy this building since before we opened. One of the conditions on our agreeing to lease here was that Tillman would give us the right of first refusal if he ever decided to sell. But he never said a word about putting the place on the market, and Hank's talked to him at least three times in the last week, let alone before that."

"If that proviso was in the lease—" I began.

"Unfortunately it's not." She scrubbed her hands through her hair. "I knew we should have formalized it, but…" She bit her lip. "I'm sorry. But I need to…" She made a vague gesture in the direction of the kitchen.

"Go, go," I said. "We can manage here. Take as long as you need."

"Absolutely," PJ said staunchly. "We'll be here when you're done in case you need to vent, but fully prepared to skedaddle if you'd rather be alone."

"Thanks, Tash. PJ. Nice to meet you, Del. I'll..." She made another vague gesture, which was alarming enough—Margaret was never anything less than decisive in everything she did. She hurried off and disappeared into the kitchen.

"I'm sorry," Del said. "I didn't mean to upset them."

"You didn't." I patted his hand, which for some reason made him blush again. "Their landlord is the culprit there. In fact, I'm sure they're grateful for the information. It gives them the opportunity to be proactive."

"Hmmm..." PJ tapped his teacup with one finger. "You said the upgrades were a condition of the sale. Could you—"

"No!" Del barked, then looked a little shamefaced. "Sorry. I mean, I'd never compromise on a contracted job. Not just professionally, but personally."

PJ scrunched up his face. "I know. Mea culpa. I shouldn't even joke about that."

"I didn't mean to snap at you, PJ." He sighed, gazing down into his teacup. "It's just that this job is turning out to be a real bear, and not just because of the state of the building."

"PJ told us you're the general contractor?" I asked, offering him the plate of scones.

"That's right." He selected a ginger and a lemon poppyseed. "It's my first gig since I got licensed in Oregon, so I shouldn't complain. But some of the subcontractors Mr. Tillman insisted on using aren't performing up to standard." He took a bite of the poppyseed scone, and his morose expression lightened. "This is delicious."

"I'll tell Margaret you liked it," I said with a smile. PJ gave me a very peculiar look—eyes popped so wide I could see the whites around his brown irises—and I mouthed, *What?*

He huffed in exasperation. "For pity's sake, Delbert, don't stop now. What kind of substandard work are we talking about? *Dish.*"

CHAPTER FOUR

Del narrowed his eyes at PJ. "If you want information, you know what you have to do. *Pete.*"

They stared at one another, and I could almost see what they must have been like as kids. Oddly enough, PJ was the one to blink first. "Fine. What kind of substandard work are we talking about, *Del*?"

Del nodded in satisfaction. "General shoddiness and an overall lack of professionalism. I had to insist the electrical sub fire one of his guys today because his work wasn't just sloppy. It was dangerous."

"Hmmm," PJ said. "I think I may have had a close encounter with that fellow on the sidewalk earlier. So ill-mannered, and orange was *not* his color."

Del polished off the poppyseed scone and reached for the ginger. "The HVAC subcontractor hasn't even shown up yet. I've had to put off the county inspector twice already."

I winced. "Ouch. Trust me, I can totally relate to working with team members who don't pull their weight."

PJ nodded. "We both do. Jensin Tech is the poster child for dysfunctional teams. It's a *Peter Principle* case study waiting to happen."

Del studied PJ, his brow furrowed. "You complain about your job all the time. Why don't you look for another one?"

"Easy." PJ leaned against me. "Tash is there. As long as it's the two of us against the bozos, we can manage."

I chuckled. "I admit I'd love to jettison the corporate world, but a girl's got to eat and pay rent. If it gets too bad, I can always decompress with a craft project or two."

"Ugh." PJ rolled his eyes. "Don't get her started on crafts, Del. You'll be here for *eons*."

Del's shy smile lit his face again. "I wouldn't mind. What crafts are you into?"

I blinked. Was he...? He couldn't be flirting with me. Could he? No... he was probably just being nice and making polite conversation to defuse the awkwardness of the unexpected introduction. "I, um..."

"What LaTashia is trying to say is that she's into *all* the crafts."

I shot him a glare. "Not *all* of them, thank you."

Del chuckled, a low, warm rumble that was light years away from Bjorn's loud, sharp bark of laughter—like the difference between tea and a boilermaker. "Don't mind PJ. He's never understood that sometimes the process of creation—or repair or deconstruction—can be just as enjoyable as the product."

"Exactly!" I beamed at him, and this time, *he* blinked.

PJ leaned back in his chair and folded his arms. "There is nothing wrong with being a *product* person. It means I'm focused on results."

"Process people get results too, Peej," I said. "But we also enjoy the journey."

"The journey, eh? That must be why Del spends so much time tinkering with his car's entrails. Only a deep and abiding love for the journey could explain why he's completely rebuilt his '66 GTO."

"The rebuild's not perfect," Del mumbled. "That model's prone to oil leaks and I haven't gotten mine plugged."

"You'll get it sorted," PJ said confidently, although a wicked glint still lurked in his eyes. "It's all part of the *journey*, after all, and you're a wizard with car innards."

"Only the '60s classic ones," Del said. "I can't handle all the computer-assisted stuff that started showing up in the seventies."

PJ leaned into me again. "What Del is too modest to tell you is that it's not just his *own* classic car journey he's embarked on. He fixes *other people's* cars too. They actually *pay* him for those particular journeys."

Del shrugged. "I like the work. And"—his bright grin split his beard— "a guy's got to eat and pay rent."

I laughed. "Touché."

"I haven't had much time since I got up here to work on my car or anybody else's. This job…" Del shook his head. "I've been doing a lot of the carpentry myself because the woodworker on Tillman's crew doesn't seem capable of cutting a decent miter joint or know how to level a chair rail."

I perked up. "You do woodworking too?"

"I'm a GC, so I can pitch in wherever I need to."

"He's being modest again," PJ sang. "He may revel in getting all greasy and sweaty with his automobile friends, but I'm convinced that his true talent lies in fine woodworking."

Woodworking was one craft I'd never really explored, and I totally admired anybody who'd mastered it. "Really?"

Del blushed again. "It's nothing."

"It is most certainly something," PJ declared. "He built the cabinets in my aunt's Craftsman bungalow, and you would *swear* they were original fixtures. He built a Victorian dollhouse for our cousin's kids *from scratch*. His inlaid puzzle boxes are better than *anything* you can find in specialty stores or online. And the Art Deco jewelry case he made for my mother—"

"PJ." Del's voice was agonized. "Please don't."

"But Del," he said, "you're brilliant. You shouldn't hide your talent under a bushel. Or a GTO chassis. Or even a construction site, for that matter."

"Like I said..." Del shared a warm glance with me. "...I've got to pay the bills, and messing around with wood isn't gonna do the trick."

"If you'd ever like to share any of your projects, Del," I said, "I'd love to see them. I'm always interested in other people's art." I glanced at the kitchen door. No sign yet of Hank or Margaret. "In fact, Margaret and I are working on something here. Would you like to see it?"

PJ clutched his hair. "Good grief, don't *encourage* her."

"Excuse me." I poked him in the shoulder. "Who just spent the weekend sourcing and cleaning pennies for this project?"

He sighed uber-dramatically. "Guilty. What can I say? I'm an enabler. On the other hand, I never claimed consistency was one of my faults."

"Isn't consistency supposed to be a virtue?" Del asked. "How else can you expect the right results?"

"It's only a virtue, my dear cousin, if you're consistent at success. Consistently inappropriate results are *always* a fault." He grimaced. "Much like my dating life."

"So you're saying you *are* consistent?" I asked with a grin.

He stuck his nose in the air. "I'm consistently inconsistent." He flapped both his hands at me in a shooing motion. "Now, don't you have a mosaic to display? I'd come along, but Del takes up a lot of real estate and I doubt that little room could hold all three of us."

I narrowed my eyes, studying PJ as he made a big production of selecting exactly the right scone. He was being conspicuously nonchalant, and that always meant he had ulterior motives. I shook my head and got to my feet. Whatever was on his mind, he'd tell me eventually. That was one of PJ's other faults—unless it counted as a virtue: While he was totally discreet with other people, he was incapable of keeping a secret from me.

Del struggled out of his chair, his hip knocking the table and rattling the teacups. He winced. "Sorry."

"No harm done." Before I led him down the hallway, I pointed out some of the other Airship Ambassador decorations. The Cheshire Cat mischievously winking down from his perch on a chandelier made from thrift store-scrounged teacups. The typewriter with the lightning orb that sat in the corner. "And of course"—I pointed at the exquisite dirigible model— "the *Firelight*."

"*Firelight*?" he asked with a smile.

"Well, Firefly was already taken, even though that was technically the spaceship's class and not its name." We walked down the short hall and stopped at the door leading to our destination. "Hank and Margaret are adding a second restroom."

"Per code," Del said, then blushed. "Sorry. Didn't mean to interrupt."

I smiled at him. "No worries. Yes, it's the result of their last inspection after they reconfigured their space. They'd intended to add it anyway, for the sake of their customers' comfort." I glanced at the kitchen door. Still no sign of Hank or Margaret. "They just obtained their liquor license, which is why they were so keen on either leasing the space next door or buying the building." I patted his arm. "They really weren't upset with you. Tillman selling the building out from under them was a pretty low blow."

He nodded as he gazed meditatively at the *Firelight* as its inner glow transitioned from green to blue to a soft purple. "I imagine. There's nothing worse than somebody who doesn't keep their promises, including their business commitments. Even if they're just handshake deals."

I studied his profile. When he wasn't being rather adorably flustered, he was remarkably resolute and obviously had serious personal and professional ethics. Of course, since he was PJ's cousin—one PJ was clearly fond of—I'd expect nothing less.

PJ had one of the strongest moral codes of anyone I knew, and he hadn't discovered it under a convenient cabbage leaf. Loyalty was one of his watchwords—particularly to his friends. I suspected Del might share the same values.

I cleared my throat. "Anyway, Margaret decided to use the *Firelight* as a model for a mosaic on the restroom floor using pennies."

He smiled down at me—and he could actually look down, something that didn't happen often, given my height and my penchant for platform shoes—and I thought I could detect a decided twinkle in his eyes. "Is that why there's a coin shortage these days?"

I laughed. So he did have a sense of humor, after all. "We may be contributing in a small way, but I doubt a couple of mosaics are the root cause."

His sandy eyebrows rose. "A couple?" Then his expression cleared. "Ah. The octopus in the other restroom. I meant to mention it when I joined you all at the table, but it, er, slipped my mind." The tips of his ears turned pink. "It's a terrific piece and works great with the whole deep sea motif." He leaned down. "Although the full-sized antique diving suit in the corner made me feel like I was being judged."

We shared a laugh. "So far, there are no potential onlookers in the new restroom, but I make no promises. Margaret likes to go all in with her decorations, and I've got some ideas for a mixed media installation in there involving airship captain hats and regalia." I crossed my arms and tapped my finger on my chin. "Definitely something with goggles."

"Yikes!" He clapped a hand over his eyes. Apparently, PJ wasn't the only one in the family with a flair for the dramatic. "I think I might have nightmares."

"Not everyone is a fan of the steampunk aesthetic."

He peeked at me from under his hand and it was... ridiculously cute. "It's not the aesthetic. I love that. It's the sightless eyes staring at me while I—" He hid his eyes again. "I'll stop talking now."

I laughed again. "Come on. Let's take a look at the project before PJ eats all the scones."

"I heard that," PJ called, "and it's your own fault for abandoning the field. Possession is nine-tenths of the law." He trotted over to join us, dusting crumbs off his fingers. "Ten-tenths when it comes to Margaret's baking."

"Don't mind him," I said. "He doesn't mean it."

Del smiled fondly down at PJ. "I know. He's solid. Always has been."

"Then let's take a look at—"

The gift shop curtain billowed toward us, followed by the rattle of glass as the outside door slammed shut. "I know you're in there! Get out here now."

CHAPTER FIVE

The voice—loud, belligerent, and completely unfamiliar— stopped me in my tracks. PJ must have forgotten to lock up behind him after he fetched Del. The scowling man who batted the curtain aside was a stranger, and I was ready to give him the usual spiel about the tearoom being closed on Mondays and Tuesdays, when I noticed that Del had gone very tense beside me. He turned slowly, and even behind the cover of his beard I could tell his jaw was set.

Judging by his muttered curse, the intruder wasn't a stranger to him.

"Mr. Jenkins," Del said, verifying my guess, "what brings you here today?"

"Oh, my word," PJ murmured. "It's the snitty guy in the unfortunate green suit."

Mr. Jenkins, a man who was so thin he could hide behind a telephone pole, was shorter than both Del and me, but probably a little taller than PJ. He clung to his clipboard like a shield as he cast a dismissive glance around the tearoom before advancing on Del. "An inspection. What else?"

Del's brow furrowed. "I didn't realize the county did surprise inspections."

Mr. Jenkins scoffed. "It's not a surprise. You scheduled it." He checked the clipboard in his hand. "Electrical and plumbing."

Del's frowned deepened. "The work's not ready for inspection yet. The electrical sub has to redo half the work to bring it up to standard. The plumbing sub is on site today, but he's waiting for fixtures to arrive later this week."

"If you're not ready—*again*—why are you wasting my time?"

"I'm not. I never scheduled—"

"It's right here." Jenkins held up the clipboard and tapped what looked like a printed web form. "The inspection was logged on the system two days ago."

"The only reason I've accessed the website for the last week was to check on the progress of the mechanical permit."

"The evidence suggests otherwise."

I bit my lip. I really wanted to eject Jenkins and his attitude from the tearoom—I didn't want his negativity encroaching on one of my happy places—but I also didn't want to interrupt and perhaps mortify Del by reminding him this conversation wasn't exactly private.

I cut a glance at PJ. Knowing him, he'd be ready to wade into the fray if it looked like Del needed backup, but neither one of us knew what this was about. The last thing I wanted to do was make things worse for Del, and I had no doubt PJ felt the same.

Del's attention never wavered from Jenkins. "Why on earth would I call for an inspection we were bound to fail?"

"A very good question, and I'm not the only one who expects a decent answer." He tucked the clipboard under his arm, a truly unpleasant smile twisting his lips. "You're only recently licensed in this state, I believe."

"That's right," Del said slowly.

"If you waste my time again, I'll be forced to inform the Construction Contractors' Board of your inability to follow protocol. Your tenure here might be shorter than you expect." He turned and stormed out.

Del's shoulders sagged and he rubbed a hand over his beard. "Well, shoot."

PJ propped his fists on his hips, glaring out at the sidewalk, where Jenkins had stopped to make a call on his cell phone. "What in the world was that dreadful little man going on about?"

Del smiled crookedly. "You're smaller than he is, Pete."

PJ switched his glare to Del. "I'm not *small*. I'm *medium*. And besides, smallness isn't defined by stature alone. That... that *person* has 'small-minded' written all over him."

Del sighed. "Unfortunately, he's the commercial building inspector for the county. So no matter how big or small his mind, ticking him off isn't in my best interests if I want to complete this job successfully."

I watched Jenkins on the sidewalk as he gesticulated wildly with his clipboard. "Why do you suppose he was so convinced about the inspections being scheduled?"

Del rubbed the back of his neck. "Beats the heck out of me. The process is all computerized now. The project has its own web page. You log in and request an inspection and the website spits out the date for you."

PJ's eyes narrowed. "Even a secure online process can be manipulated under the right conditions."

"Yeah? Like what?" Del asked.

"By someone who has the right login credentials, of course. So tell me, Delbert"—PJ fluttered his eyelashes— "who else has the credentials to log in to your job?"

"Well..." Del screwed up his face in thought. "The people at Mr. Tillman's office, I guess. He's got a couple of assistants who handle logistics for him. Each of the subcontractors has access to their own area, too."

"Tillman's a weasel, and you've fired more than one sub, I believe, so suspects abound." PJ executed a little bow, complete with hand flourish. "Gentlefolk of the jury, I rest my case."

"The subs I can see," Del said. "They weren't too happy. But Mr. Tillman wants to get this project done just like I do. Granted, he'd prefer it to get done sooner than I think is possible because he's got the buyer breathing down his neck, but annoying the county inspectors won't make things go any faster."

"Could be he's just got incompetent people working for him. But maybe"—PJ drew out the word, tapping his chin contemplatively—"your ideas about project completion don't jibe with his. I know you, Delbert. You want the job done *right*. Maybe Tillman just wants the job *done*."

"I suppose." Del sighed and trudged over to retrieve his tool belt. "Maybe it's his way of trying to... to..."

"Kick you in the butt?" PJ said helpfully.

"I was going to say move things along, but one way or another, Jenkins is right. I need to get back to work." He fastened the belt around his waist. "No telling what that electrical sub will try to pull if I'm not there to keep an eye on him." He gave PJ a hug—and not just a one-armed, back-slapping bro hug either, which told me their relationship was based on real affection—and then turned to me. "It was great meeting you at last, Tash." He shrugged apologetically. "Sorry I'll miss seeing the mosaic in progress, but maybe I can catch the finished product sometime soon."

"Anytime." I shook his hand. "I'd love to hear more about your woodworking projects, too. And if you're available to take commissions, I may need to hire you to make some small shadowboxes for me."

The tips of his ears pinked again, but he nodded and then strode out of the shop. Unlike Jenkins, who'd punctuated his exit with a slam that rattled the windows, Del shut the door gently behind him. Unfortunately, that didn't let him escape from Jenkins, because the man peremptorily gestured Del over to him and proceeded to brandish his clipboard some more while Del regarded him stonily, arms crossed.

The swinging kitchen door *whumph*ed closed behind us and Margaret appeared by my side. I glanced down at her. Her expression was nearly as grim as Del's.

"Did you get hold of Tillman?"

"No," Margaret said, her tone laced with disgust. "But Hank left him a *very* pointed voicemail." She squinted at the scene on the sidewalk. "And speaking of angry, who was that jerk who just left?"

PJ bristled. "I hope you're not referring to my cousin."

"Not the smitten teddy bear," Margaret said with a sly glance in my direction. "The other guy."

"Mr. Jenkins," PJ said, as if he were announcing that Hannibal Lecter would be joining us for tea. "The county inspector."

Her eyebrows shot up. "County inspector? As in the guy who's got the final say over whether the sale goes through?"

"Well, he certainly has a major say," I said, "since the new owner couldn't get approved for occupancy until he signs off on it. He's the one who'll attest that the upgrades to the building were done to code."

"So he's supposed to be impartial, right?" she asked, eyes narrowing. "Only concerned with building codes and safety?"

"Yes," I said slowly as Del turned and walked away from Jenkins whose face had gone an alarming purple.

"Then what was he doing cozied up at the Three Sombreros sharing a platter of nachos and a pitcher of margaritas—" She shifted her weight to one side and propped her fist on her hip. "—with Jeffrey-flipping-Tillman?"

CHAPTER SIX

Expecting the mosaic to take us at least two days to complete, I'd arranged both Monday and Tuesday off work. Margaret and Hank were still trying to chase down Tillman on Tuesday, though, so I had the day free to plan a series of gothic shadowboxes for the gift shop and sort through the mountain of craft supplies I'd inherited after my friend Ava's passing.

That second item wasn't exactly a cakewalk, either. My own craft room had been neat but stuffed to the gills *before* Ava's daughter had gifted me with her mother's inventory. Since Ava had an eye for both quality and quantity, my apartment looked like Michael's and Dick Blick had birthed a love child smack in the middle of a gigantic estate sale. *Three* gigantic estate sales.

As a result, at the office on Wednesday, I had what PJ referred to as one of my craft hangovers. I was still visualizing everything I wanted to create, and as a result, I lost track of time and had to rush to an all-company meeting with only minutes to spare.

PJ was waiting for me outside the big conference room that we normally used for training. He was wearing his usual hipster-geek work outfit: black skinny jeans, rainbow suspenders, white button-down, and a TARDIS bow tie.

He cocked an eyebrow at me. "Well, well, well. Isn't this a turn-up for the books?"

"What? My outfit?" I glanced down at my black swing dress covered with vibrant green cacti paired with a wide red belt and matching cardigan the same red as the blooms on the cacti. "You think I should lose the belt?"

"Are you kidding?" He sniffed. "The belt totally makes the outfit."

My phone—my personal cell, not my work phone—vibrated in my dress pocket. Ordinarily, I wouldn't check it except during lunch or breaks—and certainly not in a company meeting—but my mind was still occupied with figurines, background papers, and tiny tombstones for the shadowboxes. "Then what are you talking about?" I asked as I pulled out the phone.

"Well, it's entirely usual for *me* to be fashionably late to these oh-so-fascinating shindigs, but you're Ms. Punctual."

I gave him an exasperated glare. "They only gave us half an hour's notice for this meeting. I was on a call with a vendor most of the morning."

"Mmmhmm," he said, not sounding at all mollified. "Yet when I walked past your office on the way to get you a cup of coffee"—he handed it over—"you're welcome, by the way, you were staring at your Lieutenant Uhura painting with your thoughts clearly in a galaxy far, far away."

I was only half paying attention because the text was from Rhonda. She'd sent me links to three different properties in my price range. A little thrill chased down my spine. I'd never expected her to work so quickly. I *knew* I was right to give her a chance. "You're mixing your geek references."

PJ waved a negligent hand. "Irrelevant. And I'd like to point out that you're checking your *personal* cell phone, *not* your work phone, something you never do when you're on the clock."

I tore my gaze away from the phone and glanced into the conference room where Neal, our CEO, was just sauntering up to the podium. "I... Um."

PJ grinned. "You're *distracted*, babycakes." He waggled his eyebrows. "Could it be because you've got something—or should I say some*body* on your mind?"

I blinked at him. "What? Who?"

"Oh, I don't know." He took a sip of his coffee. "A certain tall, bearded blond who got flustered every time he so much as glanced your way? Although I confess, I didn't think he'd managed to score your digits."

My phone buzzed again, and I simply had to take a peek. Rhonda again. "You mean Del?"

"Who else? You haven't been meeting any other tall, bearded blonds lately, have you? Wait." He grasped my wrist so he felt the next text vibrate, too. "Bjorn isn't sniffing around here again, is he?"

I checked out the room again. Neal was chatting quietly with a man I didn't recognize, but the meeting was bound to start soon. "No, Bjorn isn't around and even if he were—"

"I know Del doesn't have that Viking physique, but—"

"Wait. Are you suggesting that I'm daydreaming about Del?"

PJ's eyebrows bunched. "Why not? He's a great guy. And he *likes* you. I can tell."

I thought back to meeting PJ's sweet cousin yesterday. "How?"

"He let you touch his *tool belt*. Nobody gets to do that. I'm just wondering..." He rocked from his heels to his toes, grinning. "...if he let you touch his *tool*, too."

"PJ!" My voice was maybe a little too loud, earning me quizzical glances from a couple of members of the design engineering team who were sitting in the back row as usual. I ducked aside from the open doorway, out of their sight, and lowered my voice. "For your information, the texts are from Rhonda. And you're right, I shouldn't have checked, but my mind was on... something else."

He slapped his hand over his eyes and groaned. "Oh, for pity's sake, you're not in love, drat it all. You're in a crafting fugue. I should know the signs by now."

I peered down at him guiltily. "Well…"

"Never mind." He took my arm and towed me inside the room. There weren't any open seats except in the center of the nearly full rows, so rather than call attention to our tardiness, we stood at the back and sipped our now tepid coffee.

Just in time, too, because Neal turned away from his conversation and faced us across the podium.

"Good afternoon, everyone." His smile was a little too wide, but Neal had a tendency to misread the crowd at the best of times. "Thank you all for coming on such short notice."

My phone buzzed again, and with a surreptitious glance at PJ, I touched the screen to bring up the message app.

RhondaR: Forget those earlier links!!! This is the perfect house for you!!!

In addition to the surplus exclamation points, she'd added at least a dozen heart emojis to her text.

At the front of the room, Neal was droning on about something, but with my perfect house potentially *right there* at my fingertips, I couldn't focus on his words. He wasn't the most dynamic speaker, even when he had thrilling news, and since PJ —that font of all office gossip—hadn't heard about anything particularly earth-shattering coming down the pike, I couldn't imagine his announcement could be that crucial. It was probably just another pitch for staff engagement—like that ridiculous Fun Committee he'd saddled me with last June.

Whatever it was, I could count on PJ to bring me up to speed later. I made sure the sound was turned down on the phone— Rhonda had been known to accompany her sales pitches with what she considered appropriate mood music—and clicked the latest link to bring up the listing.

The first picture was… not particularly exciting. It was a single story, the facade painted a nondescript gray with a wide picture window on one side of the door and two smaller windows on the other side, making it look a little lopsided, like it was squinting one eye and opening the other wide. I sighed, Neal's voice nothing but white noise in my ears. What would make Rhonda think this house was perfect for me? Granted, my budget wasn't enormous, but it was respectable. I'd been saving for this moment for years.

I cast a quick glance at Neal. He hadn't brought out any pie charts or line graphs, so he wasn't talking about poor sales performance or product defects, the only things I really needed to worry about. I tapped on the next picture, another street-view shot. The front yard was a neat rectangle of green, and the sidewalk leading to the door was lined with wilting pansies. A long driveway led to what looked like a single-car garage set back from the house.

Still not wowing me. I scrolled down to the next image and… okay now *that* was a *wow!* My gasp must have been louder than I realized, because not only did I draw the attention of everyone in the back half of the room, but Neal glanced at me as he relinquished his spot at the podium to the other man whose name I hadn't caught.

But who could blame me? Now I knew why Rhonda thought this house was perfect for me. The link was an interactive 360 view of the most perfect craft room I'd ever seen. It had to run easily half the width of the house, with wide windows overlooking a vast back yard bordered with mature trees. A built-in work counter, a wall rack for rolls of wrapping paper and ribbons, a corner sewing machine table, and space for additional shelving and storage. It even had running water right in the room—there was a sink in the corner.

Frankly, I didn't care if the rest of the place was a dump. Okay, maybe I cared a little bit. But I could forgive a lot for a craft room like this, and I could always renovate if the other rooms were subpar. There was plenty of room to build out in the back, and with a single story, I could always go up, too, right? It was in Tualatin, a little farther from work than I liked, but *craft room!* I could check out the building codes later for expansion possibilities. I just had to see the whole thing.

I grinned when Rhonda sent another text with a list of appointment times for us to view the place. My grin faded when I realized none of the options were sooner than this weekend, but maybe I could drive by it beforehand with PJ to check out the neighborhood. I was sure he'd want to—

A smattering of applause broke me out of my preoccupation. Was the meeting over already? Everyone was rising from their seats, obscuring my view of Neal and the other speaker.

"Well, that explains a lot," PJ muttered.

"What explains what?" I wanted to show him the pictures of *my* house, but not here.

"Why Vinh had us busting our little geek tushies for the last two days to clear out old equipment that's been gathering dust in our storage room forever." We queued up behind the design engineering squad who were blocking the door, looking a little shell-shocked. "Since he's successfully ignored it as long as I've known him, I knew something had to be up. I must have made more trips to Free Geek in the last two days than in the last two years."

As I glanced around the slowly emptying room, I noticed a lot of very worried expressions. "Um, Peej? What exactly did I miss?"

He raised his eyebrows. "Really, LaTashia? You missed *everything*?"

"Well…" I brandished my phone helplessly, but quickly tucked it in my pocket when I spotted Neal bearing down on us.

"Tash." Neal stopped in front of me and started doing that thing—snapping his fingers and then driving one fist into the opposite palm, his usual tell when he was unsure of his reception. "I want you to know that this shouldn't affect you much at all. With your work in marketing and all you do with the Fun Committee, now is precisely the time to celebrate and hold on to our *fun* company culture." He gave a patronizing chuckle. "The community garden wasn't the best, but— Jerry! A moment, if you don't mind." He strode off.

I frowned, bewildered. "What exactly isn't going to affect me? And that stupid garden was his idea. I tried to tell him that I'm a crafter *not* a gardener. I literally have two brown thumbs."

"For pity's sake, is your crafting fugue *that* intense?"

"It wasn't crafts. Not this time." I narrowed my eyes at him. "And before you jump to any more conclusions, it's not Del, either."

He frowned. "What's wrong with Del?"

"Nothing. But never mind. What was this meeting about?"

"Well, my dear Tash, Vernin & Sizemore has just merged with us."

I blinked, my shoulder colliding with the doorjamb as I tried to make sense of his words. "What?"

V&S was our major competitor. My team in marketing always joked that V&S actually stood for *Vicious & Sinister*. Their documentation was purposely vague, they were known for dropping prices to gain market share, and they'd been kicked off dozens of jobs, whose foremen then contracted with us to clean up the mess.

A large part of my job was positioning our products as superior to theirs, and since I was generally successful, I couldn't imagine that V&S would welcome me with open arms. In fact, their product line manager always gave me the stink-eye at conferences and trade shows, and purposely avoided speaking with me.

"We'd just gotten our new accounting system up and running. Now we'll have to figure out how to integrate with theirs," PJ grumbled.

"When you say *merged*, is this an equal partnership, or did we acquire them?"

"That... was not specified." His frowned deepened as he shoved his hands in his pockets. "It's possible that *they* acquired *us.* Neal promised more information later, but he didn't give any hints about what constitutes *later* or what the information might be. Given his Joker-sized grin, I suspect his bank account stands to gain few more commas and zeroes when the deal is done."

"Did you see this coming?" I tried not to sound accusatory, but judging from PJ's outraged expression, I'm not sure I succeeded.

"Of course not. If I had, you would have been the first to know."

I took a few deep breaths and glanced down at my phone. The screen had gone dark, hiding the craft room picture. I hoped it wasn't an omen. Neal had been known to blow smoke before. Was my job really secure? Maybe this wasn't the best time to commit to such a major purchase and life change. I checked my watch. Since I usually clocked in earlier than most people on my team, including Neal, four o'clock wasn't too early to bail, was it?

Maybe cutting out early wasn't the best political move, given that my job may or may not be in jeopardy, but I wasn't sure I could focus on anything more today, anyway. "Tea," I croaked. "I need tea." Plus a little craft therapy, and working on Margaret's mosaic would check both boxes.

"That sounds like an excellent plan. I just need to grab my messenger bag. Meet you in the parking lot in—" PJ grimaced as his own cell phone buzzed. He checked the message. "Drat. I've been summoned." He waggled his phone. "A transition meeting with the Vicious & Sinister IT department."

"Already? But they just announced it."

He gave a long-suffering sigh. "Apparently, we're the last to know. The meeting is at the V&S offices, which doesn't fill me with confidence about how the rest of this 'merger' is going to go." He patted my arm. "I'm not sure how long I'll be, so you'll have to imbibe without me today. Do give Margaret and Hank my best." He paused in the doorway. "And please, by all that's holy, don't tell me you need more freaking *pennies*."

CHAPTER SEVEN

As it happened, I wasn't able to leave early after all. Neal stopped by my office with more finger-snapping-fist-punching vague-splaining, so by the time I reached the tearoom parking lot, it was close to six o'clock with dusk rapidly approaching. A car was just pulling out as I arrived, and I glanced in my rearview as it disappeared around the corner. A gold GTO. 1966. Mint condition. *Nice*. I'd never noticed it here before.

As I parked my own sensible Honda CR-V, I wondered why the car had snagged my attention, but shook my head as I gathered my Irregular Choice Time for Tea purse and black vegan leather moto jacket from the passenger seat, dismissing it as product identification, since Del had mentioned rebuilding his own GTO on Monday. In fact, that might have been him just now. I hadn't gotten a clear view of the driver, but it had definitely been a man whose profile had been blurred by facial hair. If Neal hadn't delayed me, we might have had a chance to chat again.

I paused as I locked my car. Why was I identifying Del's... product, as it were, and regretting a missed encounter? I shrugged. Probably just a reaction to PJ's rather obvious attempt at matchmaking. I chuckled while I walked around the Magic Meatball Italian restaurant to get to the sidewalk that passed in front of the Airship Ambassador. Usually, PJ was highly critical of anybody I dated. He was absolutely scathing about Bjorn, although considering subsequent events, I probably should have listened to his dire warnings. He'd never actively tried to set me up with anybody specific, though.

I pondered Del's soft-looking beard, wavy hair, and shy smile. PJ could certainly have done worse playing Cupid, but I had too much on my plate right now—the house, the company merger, expanding my product line in the tearoom gift shop—to think about dating. Time enough to tackle that after my life settled down a bit.

My steps slowed to a stop. The door to the former Rip Snorter was ajar. I frowned. Surely if Del was headed home for the day, he would have locked up. Could one of the subcontractors be working late? One way or another, leaving the door open with night coming on wasn't the best move. This neighborhood was fine—a business district, although not all the businesses were as high end as the Airship Ambassador, the former Rip Snorter being a case in point. But leaving the site unsecured was a sure-fire way to invite unexpected and unsavory guests inside. Just look at what happened at the tearoom on Monday. That building inspector was about as unsavory as you could get when it came to attitude.

As I passed the tearoom, the gift shop was dark, but a light spilled out from the hallway, casting odd shadows in the dim dining room. I was a little surprised. The place was usually booked solid on Wednesdays, but then I remembered: The Needhams had closed the place all week to complete the restroom build-out. Margaret must still be hard at work on the mosaic. *Good.* I could offer to help. But first, I'd pop my head in next door and warn the crew about keeping the place closed up.

I pushed the door open a little wider and peeked in. Inside, it was even darker than the tea shop. "Hello? Is anybody here?" Something tickled my alarm circuits. An odor like warm iron filings, conjuring memories of my undergraduate mechanical engineering machine shop lab, hung in the air. Since there wasn't a metal workshop in a ten-mile radius, the smell could only be one thing, one I'd become more familiar with lately than I liked.

Blood.

And mixed with it, burning the back of my throat, the distinct stench of melted electrical wire.

Calm down, Tash. It's a construction site. This could be perfectly innocent. Maybe one of the workers had a minor accident. Maybe the electrical contractor had been soldering connections all afternoon. I dug in my purse for my Maglite Mini. Despite the chills creeping down my back, I couldn't help but hear PJ's voice in my head: *"An industrial-strength flashlight, LaTashia? Of course you'd have one."*

I played the beam around the floor. Plumber's tools, a bundle of PVC pipe, a nail gun, and a stack of drywall sheets lined one wall. A table saw stood in the center of the room, with a router mounted on another work bench next to it. Lengths of milled wood were arranged neatly between the tools. *That must be the molding Del told us about.* Big spools of electrical wire were lined up next to the opposite wall, along with some lengths of galvanized duct as big around as PJ's waist.

What I could see of the floor around the power tools was swept clean, so whatever else anyone could say about Del, he kept his job site in good shape. I sniffed again and took another couple of steps inside. The Rip Snorter's old bar had been torn out, exposing a swath of the plywood subfloor that was almost garish against the dark plank flooring.

"Hello?" I called again. Underneath my voice's weird echo, I caught the sound of running water and a *snap-crackle-buzz* that lifted the hair on my nape. *Live wire.* My flashlight glinted off a puddle that was spreading out of the dark hallway, pooling around the old bar top that was leaning against the rear wall.

And at its base…

I peered through the darkness, phantom caterpillars creeping up my spine. That wasn't a roll of tar paper. It wasn't a roll of insulation. It wasn't a pile of discarded rags. My stomach roiled, because I knew exactly what it was, even without seeing the pale face with its blank, empty eyes.

It was a body. And it was most definitely dead.

CHAPTER EIGHT

While my current job depended more on my MBA skills, I was also a mechanical engineer who worked for a company that designed power metering equipment. I knew better than to go anywhere near a body lying in a puddle near a suspected live wire. And as much as I hated to admit it, I absolutely knew the drill for reporting a dead body by now.

I stepped outside onto the sidewalk where the streetlights were playing chicken with the twilight. I pulled out my phone and dialed 9-1-1.

"9-1-1. What's your emergency?"

"Hello. My name is Tash Van Buren, and I've just found a man whom I believe is deceased." I gave her the address.

"Help is on the way, Ms. Van Buren. Please stay on the line with me."

"Of course."

"Can you tell if he's breathing?"

"No. And I can't really go back and check. He's lying in water, and I suspect there's a live electrical wire nearby. Even if there's no further risk of electrocution, there may be some fire danger. I don't think it's wise for me to go inside again."

"Please stay safe. Police and the fire department are on their way."

Sure enough, sirens were already approaching, which wasn't surprising. The fire station was only a few blocks away. The local police station wasn't much farther, but this had *suspicious death* written all over it—as I knew a little too well for my liking —so the medical examiner and the homicide detectives would probably take a little longer, since they had to come all the way from Hillsboro.

While I kept up a random conversation with the operator so she'd know I was still on the line, I checked the street. It was mostly deserted at this time of day. The entrance to the Magic Meatball was around the corner, and the dinner crowd usually didn't start arriving until later, anyway. Most of the other businesses on the street—like the bakery halfway down the block, the insurance office across the way, and the auto body shop on the other side of the Rip Snorter—closed by five.

Margaret. Hank. Oh, my stars. If a fire really *did* break out in the Rip Snorter, then it could spread to the tearoom. My heart pounded in my chest as I raced to the tearoom's door. It was locked, but I jiggled the handle and pounded on the wooden frame, hoping Margaret would hear me all the way back in the rear of the store.

"Listen, could I put you on hold for a minute?" I asked the operator.

"I'd really rather you stayed on the line."

"I promise I won't cut the call. But my friend is working in the tea shop next door and doesn't realize that she could be in danger." I banged on the door some more, and when that still got no response, marched to the gift shop display windows and rapped my knuckles against the glass.

"Can't you go inside the shop to alert her?"

"It's closed and the door is locked. I need to call her." The sirens got closer, and the fire engine nosed around the corner. "The fire department is here. Can't I—"

"Please wait for the police. If you give me her number, we'll make the call from here."

I took a shaky breath, every instinct urging me to just hang up and make the call. But I'd also learned that not following the instructions of emergency personnel and first responders was a terrific way to incriminate yourself. I gave her Margaret's cell number and tried my best not to bite my fingernails.

The fire engine pulled up to the curb and the firefighters leaped into action. I took a moment to imagine what PJ would say about missing the opportunity to ogle the men in their turnout gear, but then decided it was much better that he wasn't here. As grateful as I'd be for his moral support, having the two of us discover yet another dead body was moving us into *Murder, She Wrote* territory.

"Ma'am." One of the firefighters stopped next to me. "If you could move a safe distance away?" He gestured down the sidewalk, beyond the Airship Ambassador, to the corner by the Magic Meatball.

"I'm the one who called 9-1-1. I smelled burned electrical wire and there's water on the floor. I'm pretty sure there's a live wire. I heard—"

"Ma'am. We need you to step away." His voice was firm, but his eyes were kind.

I nodded numbly, still holding the phone to my ear, but as I stumbled past the tearoom, Margaret burst out of the gift shop door. Her eyes were wild, and her hair had completely escaped her bun. She wiped her hands on her chambray camp shirt, which was already blotched with something dark—probably paint.

"Tash? What's going on?"

I winced. I knew this drill too. As first on the scene, I was responsible for providing information to the police, and they wouldn't thank me for tainting the perceptions of other potential witnesses. But for now, that was a secondary concern. "Hank. Is he still inside?"

"What?" she said, not really looking at me as the firefighters rushed into the Rip Snorter.

"You need to get Hank out. There could be fire danger." I could at least say that much—the presence of the fire engine was a big freaking clue.

She tore her gaze away from the swirling red and white lights on the fire truck and looked up at me, eyes wide. "Fire? The Rip Snorter—"

"Never mind the Rip Snorter. The firefighters will handle it." Hopefully without the need to damage the tearoom's irreplaceable antiques, especially since no fire had broken out. Yet.

A police cruiser pulled up behind the fire engine and a couple of uniformed officers got out. One of them came to me while the other rushed over to speak to the firefighter whose helmet identified him as the captain. "Are you Ms. Van Buren?" she asked.

"I am." I held my phone to my ear. "The police are here now. Is it all right if I hang up?"

"Yes," the operator said. "Thank you and please stay safe."

I turned to the officer, but before she could ask anything more, a dark sedan pulled up behind the cruiser with the medical examiner's van right behind.

Margaret stared from the ME's van, to the cruiser, to the fire engine, and back to me. "I'm guessing they're not here because there's a cat up a tree."

I shook her arm as two very familiar people emerged from the sedan. "Margaret, focus. This is important. Is Hank inside?"

She shook her head. "He left earlier, to try to corner Tillman again."

My shoulders sagged with relief. "Thank goodness."

The officer stepped back, deferring to the sedan's occupants: a straight-backed woman with a salt and pepper bob and an austere man who PJ swore was a ringer for John Cho—and whom he continued to refer to as Detective Hottie.

Detective Sarah Huber smiled at me. "Tash. I hope you're well." She glanced at the fire engine and then at the ME techs striding by in their protective gear. "As well as can be expected under the circumstances, in any case."

"Ms. Van Buren." Detective Cameron Bae nodded curtly, then began to scan the area with narrowed eyes.

Margaret regarded me with a *what-the-heck* expression. "Wow. PJ's right. You really do know everybody."

I flashed on Del's smile, superimposed with the GTO with its bearded driver leaving the scene right before I discovered the body. "No. I don't think I do. Not really."

"Tash," Huber said, "you were first on the scene?"

"Yes."

"And this is..." She cocked an eyebrow at Margaret, but I noticed she gave Bae a nudge with her elbow, causing him to glance at her irritably before peering around the street.

"Oh, I'm sorry. Detective Huber, this is my friend, Margaret Needham. She and her husband Hank run the Airship Ambassador Tearoom & Apothecary." I gestured toward the shop, which was still dark except for the light leaking out from the hallway.

Huber inclined her head. "Ms. Needham. I'd like to ask you a few questions, if you don't mind, while my partner"—her elbow in Bae's ribs was a little sharper this time, judging by his wince—"talks with Tash."

"Oh." Was that panic flickering across Margaret's face? I couldn't tell in the uncertain light from the streetlamps. "All right." She and Huber retreated to stand next to the detectives' car. *Yeah, I know that drill too.*

I turned to Bae who was peering into the sparse crowd that had gathered, probably in response to all the emergency personnel who hadn't exactly arrived unobtrusively. "Detective?"

He jerked his attention to me. "Hmmm? Yes." He settled his jacket on his shoulders. "You were first on the scene?"

"Yes. I made the 9-1-1 call."

"Could you describe the events, please?"

So I did—at least about finding the Rip Snorter door ajar and discovering the body inside. A knot in my stomach twisted and tightened when I didn't mention seeing what I assumed was Del's car leave. But technically I hadn't seen *him*, and the parking lot was used by several businesses on the block, including Magic Meatball, the tea shop, and the small fine arts gallery that seemed to always be open but never have patrons.

"What was your purpose in coming to this part of town to enter a business clearly closed for renovation?"

I glared at him. "I didn't come here to go into the Rip Snorter." I gestured to the Airship Ambassador. "Margaret and I are working on a project. A mosaic on the floor of their new restroom. We were planning to finish it, but when I arrived, I noticed the bar's door was ajar and wanted to let the crew know that it wasn't a good idea, since anybody walking by might go in."

"Anybody walking by," he said, his tone dryer than my Aunt Nan's overly salted pound cake. "Such as yourself."

I took a deep breath. "Detective Bae, I am a frequent visitor to the Airship Ambassador. I bring a large party of friends to every one of their themed tea events. Margaret and Hank are personal friends, and they sell my crafts in their gift shop. I happened to be here because of my relationship with them. This also happens to be the first time I've ever set foot inside the Rip Snorter—the former Rip Snorter, I should say. It wasn't really my kind of place."

"That's right. Martini Blues, wasn't it?"

I blinked at him. "What?"

"Your kind of place. Martini Blues."

"Yes." Interesting that he should remember what my destination had been the first time we met. But he was a detective. It was his job to notice and remember details. "The Airship Ambassador is my kind of place too."

"Did you recognize the victim?"

I swallowed thickly. *Victim.* No matter how many bodies I discovered—and I fervently hoped this would be the last—I couldn't get used to that word. It was so... so judgmentally final.

"I didn't get a very close look at him. I was standing just inside the door, and he was all the way across the room against the far wall. Plus, it was dark, and I didn't want to linger because I could smell the burned electrical wire and was afraid of fire or electrocution."

"Then how were you able to make him out at all?"

I pulled my Maglite out of my purse. "With this. It's got a powerful beam, but it's very narrow. So I saw the puddle. The wire. His—" I had to swallow again. "His face." The pale skin. The wide, staring eyes, the... the... Something tickled my memory. Something recent.

"And you were alone?" Bae's sharp tone knocked the memory right out of my head. "Nobody was with you?"

"No. I mean, no, there was nobody with me. Margaret was still inside the tearoom since I hadn't let her know I'd arrived yet."

"But nobody arrived with you?"

I peered at him in the uncertain shadows. "I came alone. Straight from work." When Bae huffed in apparent disappointment, I finally got it. *He's looking for PJ.* I hid a smirk, tempted to ask who Bae was expecting. Wait until I told PJ that Detective Hottie was disappointed not to see him.

At another death scene.

Okay, maybe I wouldn't mention PJ's name. It was peculiar enough that I was first on the scene again. The last thing we needed was for more suspicion to fall on PJ. He'd already gotten a completely unfair written reprimand from Vinh for being falsely arrested, for heaven's sake.

"They're ready for us inside, Cam. Are you finished there?" Huber called.

"For now," he answered. He gave me his wintry smile. "We'll contact you if we need more."

He and Huber disappeared inside the bar. It looked as though the firefighters were preparing to leave as Margaret joined me. She looked a little shaken. I could understand that—being questioned by homicide detectives was no picnic.

I linked my arm with hers. "You okay?"

"Yeah." She stared off into the distance, not seeming to focus on anything in particular. "But I wish I knew where Hank was. I didn't expect him to be gone so long."

I peered down at her. "Are you worried that something's happened to him?"

"I don't know." She waved a hand in front of her face as though she could fend off the tears that were glistening in her eyes. "Maybe? But that detective seemed awfully interested in knowing where we've both been, and what our relationship is with the bar owner." Her breath caught, half laugh, half sob. "But we don't even know who the new bar owner *is*. In fact, I told her there might not *be* a new bar owner." She bit her lip. "I may have mentioned that we were a little annoyed about Tillman selling the building out from under us. But that doesn't mean Hank had anything to do with... with"—she gestured to the Rip Snorter, just as the ME techs wheeled out a gurney with a body bag on top—"with *this*."

"I'm sure they don't think you do." I patted her hand, but from the look she shot me, she wasn't buying my reassurance. For that matter, I wasn't sure I bought it either. Not that I'd ever think Hank, of all people, would commit any violent acts, even though he had been in the military and was still more than capable of facing a perceived threat with a threat of his own. But I could definitely see how the detectives might interpret the Needhams' feud with their landlord.

Now that I thought of it, I realized I'd never seen Jeffrey Tillman before, at least not that I was aware. Could the dead man be him? If so, that would probably make the police look a lot harder at Hank and Margaret.

If only I'd been able to leave the office when I'd wanted. Maybe I couldn't have stopped the death—whether it was accident or murder—but I could have at least given Hank and Margaret an alibi.

Assuming Bae and Huber would accept my word anymore.

"Tash?" I turned at the sound of the low, rumbly voice to find Del staring at me from the corner. He surveyed the swirling mass of people and flashing lights, dropped his tool belt, and rushed over to us. His wide brow was creased with concern as he studied me. "Are you okay? What's going on?"

"I'm fine." I moved a little closer to Margaret. I still couldn't quite believe Del would hurt anyone deliberately, but what did I really know about him, after all? "There's been an... an accident."

"Accident?" His brows drew together, and he morphed from sweetly concerned to problem-solver in a heartbeat. His gaze tracked the ME team as they slammed the rear door of their van and the cluster of firefighters readying their rig to depart. "At the job site." It wasn't a question. "Someone died."

"Yes."

Even in the sketchy light I could tell that he paled. "Who was it?"

"I don't know." I could say that truthfully, although even if I did know, I couldn't have said anything to either one of them. Not until Bae or Huber told me it was okay to discuss details.

"Where are the—" Del's gaze shifted from me to something beyond my shoulder. His mouth flattened into a thin line and he turned red.

CHAPTER NINE

"Del? Is something…"

I turned to follow the direction of his gaze and spotted a woman who reminded me of Velma from the Scooby Doo cartoons, except instead of Velma's signature orange turtleneck, she was wearing a brown blazer over a white shirt, dark jeans, and practical shoes. She was standing on the sidewalk across the street from us, directly under a streetlamp. If she'd wanted to be seen, she'd certainly accomplished her goal. I wouldn't have been surprised if she'd been observing the first responders —that's what everyone else was doing, after all. But her attention was laser-focused elsewhere.

On Del.

I glanced back at him as she strolled across the street. "Do you know her?"

He nodded curtly. "Damn ambulance chaser," he muttered.

The woman reached us, her smile like a barracuda circling a very tasty tuna. "I don't chase all the ambulances, Purdy. Only the ones spawned by you and your shoddy construction practices."

Del took an audible breath through his nose. "Did you follow me up here from Hermosa, or did you just *happen* to be in the neighborhood?"

"Get over yourself," she said. "Not everything is about you." She turned her smile on Margaret and me and it lost a little of its edge. She held out her hand. "I'm Kathryn Burns. Kate. And you are?"

"Don't tell her anything," Del growled. "Not unless you want to be smeared all over the internet."

"Really, Purdy. Innocent people shouldn't be worried about the truth, should they?"

"You don't care about truth. All you care about is—"

"Del." I put a hand on his arm, which made him startle, although he didn't move away. "It's okay."

"Do tell, Purdy. *Is* it okay?" Kate smirked, which didn't exactly endear her to me. "That's not what my witness says."

Del's frown deepened. "What witness?"

She waved a hand airily. "You'd be surprised at the incriminating information your crews are willing to share. Although I certainly wasn't. Not with your record."

I glanced between Kate and Del. "I'm not sure—"

"What are you even doing here, Kate?" Del ran a hand through his hair, but it flopped in a sandy wave over his forehead. "Don't you have enough real estate scams in Cali to keep you busy?"

"That's the thing about real estate," she drawled. "It's finite, and So Cal has less available for development now than this lovely state. So I thought I'd give Oregon a look-see. California will still be there when I get back, as will crooked developers. Although it's down one shady general contractor now."

"Excuse me," I said, because Del looked in imminent danger of an aneurism, "but who are you exactly?"

She turned to me with a flip of her dark brown hair. "We were interrupted before, weren't we? So rude. I'm Kate Burns, reporter for *Realty Reports.*"

"I've never heard of *Realty Reports.*" I shrugged. "Sorry." If it wasn't related to crafts, the power distribution industry, or one of the many fandoms PJ and I followed religiously, I was less likely to know about it.

She didn't seem insulted by my lack of familiarity, though. Instead, she pulled a business card out of her blazer pocket. "We do online investigative reporting on residential and commercial real estate. We focus on real estate law, construction safety, and urban planning."

I perked up a little at that. "I'm looking at buying my first house. Would your site help with that?"

She gave a little headshake. "We're more on the other end—construction and development, either commercial or large scale residential, not individual home buyers. But"—she shot a sly sidelong glance at Del—"you can still learn a lot about potential problems or what kinds of developers and contractors to avoid."

The muscles in Del's arm tensed under my hand, so before he could respond to her obvious insinuation, I jumped in. "Have you moved to Oregon, then?"

She scoffed. "Not likely. I just follow the stories. Since we're an online company, we can live where we want."

Margaret and I exchanged glances. Margaret was an Oregon native, and while I was a transplant from Ohio, I loved my adopted state. Kate had just lost a couple more points in my book.

I pasted on a smile and gestured to the street with its mismatched collection of storefronts. "Then what brings you here? We don't exactly have a huge commercial footprint."

"Oh, I don't know," she said with another smirk. "As a watchdog agency, we consider no story too small if its fallout stands to affect a larger audience."

"You mean no story is too small if it feeds your obsession," Del muttered.

Kate's expression turned downright murderous. "It's not an obsession when a gross injustice has been perpetrated. When shoddy construction practices and criminal safety violations occur at—"

"Excuse me. What criminal safety violations?" All of us turned at the sound of Detective Bae's sharp question. He turned his intense gaze on Kate. "Who *are* you?"

She smiled toothily at him and held out her hand, but Bae didn't shake it, nor did he lose his usual stoic aplomb. "Kate Burns. I'm a reporter for *Realty Reports*."

Bae's mouth firmed even more. "How are you associated with this incident?"

"I'm a reporter. Providing the public with crucial information is what I do."

Bae's eyebrow canted a fraction of an inch. "What crucial information do you expect to find here? As the lead detective, I have no statement for the press at this time."

Kate jutted her chin out, losing her affability. "The public has a right to know—"

"The public doesn't have the right to interfere with an ongoing investigation, and neither do you. I must ask you to leave, or at least move beyond the scene perimeter."

She gestured to Margaret, Del, and me. "They're allowed to stand here. I have a right to stand here, too."

"Two of them are material to the investigation." Bae fixed Del with his thousand-yard stare. "Who are you?"

"I'm the general contractor in charge of the renovations for the bar. Del Purdy."

Bae's gaze sharpened. "Purdy?"

"Del," I said brightly, "this is Detective Bae. PJ might have mentioned him to you after our adventure last June." I turned to Bae. "Del is PJ's cousin. He's recently moved to town."

Kate snorted. "Wonder how long until he's run out of this one, too."

Del's tension ramped up by a factor of ten. The muscles in his arm were like concrete, and he clenched his jaw so hard I was surprised his molars didn't splinter.

Bae stared impassively at Kate, not saying anything, until she blinked first, breaking eye contact and becoming suddenly interested in the cracks in the sidewalk.

"Please step away, Ms. Burns," Bae said. "I will have an officer escort you if you don't leave voluntarily."

Her head jerked up, and her eyes narrowed. "There's such a thing as freedom of the press, you know." She jabbed a finger in Del's direction. "And why aren't you making him leave? Just because he's somehow related to somebody you know?"

Bae gestured to one of the officers. "Freedom of the press relates to what you're allowed to print. It doesn't give you unlimited access to everything, particularly when you could compromise an investigation. And"—his glare was positively glacial—"I don't need to justify how I run my investigations to you. Officer Ramirez, will you please escort Ms. Burns outside the active scene perimeter?"

"Sure thing, Detective." Ramirez grinned at me. "Hi, Tash."

"Officer Ramirez," I said with a smile. He'd been very sweet to me after PJ and I found poor Ava, helping me out of an Adirondack chair when my favorite Breakfast at Tiffany's dress made it impossible for me to rise on my own. "Nice to see you. I didn't realize you'd transferred to the Beaverton PD."

Del gave Ramirez the once-over. Did he really straighten his shoulders and puff out his chest? I needed PJ here to interpret male confrontational behavior for me.

Kate glared at me this time. "This whole thing stinks of police corruption and favoritism. Everyone here is just a little too cozy. You'll be hearing from me."

Officer Ramirez's smile disappeared, and I swore the temperature in the immediate area dropped a few degrees. "This way, Ms. Burns. Now, if you please."

Bae waited until Officer Ramirez had accompanied Kate to where the rest of the onlookers were gathered, then he turned to Del. "You're the GC for this job?"

Del nodded. "That's right." He moved closer to me until his arm bumped mine. I wasn't sure if it was for his reassurance or mine.

"How well do you know Donald Jenkins?"

"Jenkins? The building inspector?"

That's the memory I'd been chasing. The victim's wide eyes and open mouth—I'd seen the same configuration of features before, although infused with anger and annoyance rather than slack in death—when he'd confronted Del in the tearoom on Monday.

"Yes," Bae said, the word clipped.

"He's the county inspector for the job, so I've talked with him a few times."

"When was the last time you saw him?"

The fire engine turned off its lights and pulled away from the curb. Del tracked its progress and clenched his jaw even tighter. "If Mr. Jenkins has a complaint about the electrical installation, I told him that we were in the process of redoing a lot of substandard work. We're not ready for the inspection yet."

"Just answer the question, please, Mr. Purdy. When did you see him last?"

"Monday," Del said with no hesitation. "At about 4:15 in the afternoon."

"That's a very precise estimate. Did you have an appointment?"

"No." Del glanced at me and blushed. "But it was right after I met Tash for the first time, so I, um, remember."

Huber, who'd joined the party shortly after Kate was evicted, glanced at how close Del and I were standing to one another and gave me a lopsided smile. "One of these days, we should play Six Degrees of Tash Van Buren. I'm convinced that you're the social center of Washington County."

Bae just sighed. "Mr. Purdy, can you tell me who has keys to the job site?"

"Just Mr. Tillman, the owner, and me, as far as I know." Del nodded his thanks to Officer Ramirez, who handed Del his discarded toolbelt. "Since I'm unfamiliar with most of the subcontractors, I prefer to keep a close eye on them. I don't want them on site without me."

I frowned in confusion. If that was the case… "Then where were you—"

"Actually…" Margaret raised her hand. "I think there may be more keys floating around out there. Tillman never changed the locks after the Rip Snorter closed. In fact," she glanced at me, her expression unreadable, "I think we had one once."

Bae frowned. "Why?"

"I'm not really sure. I'd have to ask Hank." She glanced between Huber and Bae. "My husband. He's the one who handled that. I think he might have been working on some kind of project for the previous owner." She spread her hands in a *what can you do* gesture. "He's good at cobbling things together."

"Very well. We'd like to speak with him."

"He's… not here right now."

This time, Bae's sigh was even more long-suffering. He handed Margaret a card. "Please have him call me. We'll have some questions. In the meantime." He turned to Del. "If you would please accompany us, Mr. Purdy? We have some things we'd like to discuss with you."

CHAPTER TEN

After Del accompanied the detectives inside the bar, I turned to Margaret. "Do you want me to stay with you for a while? I know this can be a shock." Yeah, unfortunately, I knew *that* all too well. My knees were still shaking. "We could work on the mosaic some more. Sometimes crafting is just what I need to take my mind off stressful situations."

She pushed her hair out of her face and shook her head. "Thank you, sweetie, but I got most of it done earlier. I'm almost ready to pour the epoxy to seal the floor. I think I'd rather call it a day." She uttered a choked laugh. "I guess it's a good thing the shop's already closed the rest of the week for the fumes to dissipate, huh?"

Bae had informed her that until they'd processed the scene completely, the Airship Ambassador couldn't open for business. "They're pretty good about not inconveniencing people unnecessarily. I'm sure they'll clear you soon since this"—I flapped one hand—"this *thing* doesn't have anything to do with you other than proximity."

"Right." She chewed on her lower lip. "I need to track Hank down and let him know what's going on." She smiled at me shakily. "But come by tomorrow after work, maybe?"

"Absolutely." I said goodbye and headed for my car.

The crowd had mostly melted away except for Kate Burns, who was watching the Rip Snorter door like a hawk. She started to follow me, but I had no desire to speak to her. There was only one person I wanted to talk to at the moment: PJ. He wasn't going to believe it when I let him know I was involved in *another* investigation.

But with Kate bearing down on me, I didn't stop to call or text him. Instead, I hurried to the parking lot, climbed into the CR-V, and headed for Tang Dynasty, PJ's favorite Chinese takeout place. After I placed the order, I sent him a text.

Tash: I've got Happy Family and G&Ts. Meet me at my place in fifteen?

I waited, but the little *delivered* icon never popped up. By the time I got home, it was clear that PJ still hadn't gotten the message and that I'd have a boatload of leftovers. *Guess lunch tomorrow is covered.* I considered the drinks and sighed. Even though the events of the day had been traumatic, I never liked drinking alone.

So after I ate, I resorted to my other decompression technique and retreated to my craft room—my extremely crowded craft room. I really, really needed a bigger place. I only hoped the company merger didn't kill my hopes for a house.

By the time I fell into bed at midnight, I'd finished three Poe-themed shadowboxes, but hadn't heard a peep from PJ. He hadn't answered any of my texts or responded to my voicemail either. I was a little concerned, but I woke up to a message that he'd sent at 3:45 a.m. that apologized for being incommunicado but gave no details. I could forgive him for that. If he'd been pulled into another one of Vinh's emergency all-nighters, he'd be exhausted and unlikely to be at work before noon.

When I arrived at the office, my first order of business was to locate Neal and make him give me the straight scoop on what the merger meant for me. In the last few months, he'd hinted about a promotion without ever saying it in so many words. Would that still be in the cards, or had our entire org chart gotten tossed out the window?

Neal's assistant, Alaia, was staring into space as she ground an inoffensive pencil into a stub in her electric sharpener.

"Good morning, Alaia. Is Neal in yet?"

She blinked up at me with a start. "Oh, Tash. Hi. I didn't see you there." She craned her neck to peer through Neal's open door to where his desk sat. "No. He's not here yet."

"Could you let him know I'd like to speak with him, please?"

"Sure thing." She picked up another pencil and shoved it relentlessly to its doom.

I gave her my best sympathetic smile. "I don't mean to pry, hon, but are you okay or have those pencils done something to offend you?"

"Oh. No." She let go of the unlucky pencil and it clattered to her desk. "I mean, no the pencils haven't offended me. But this merger is... I just don't know what's going *on*." Her voice rose in a wail, and she clapped her hands over her mouth, gaze darting to Neal's door. When he didn't pop out like a finger-snapping Jack-in-the-box, she dropped her hands and snatched up a little metal figurine with a brass nut for a head and a washer for a skirt. She didn't meet my eyes as she toyed with it. "I usually know about stuff because, well, you know Neal."

"I do," I said dryly.

"Exactly!" She set the little figure down again. "I keep him organized. But he hasn't told me *anything*. I mean, is my job safe? Is anybody's?"

As much as I wanted to find out about my own future, I couldn't add to Alaia's stress. "I'm sure you'll be fine. Neal couldn't manage without you."

She looked up at me, brown eyes hopeful. "You really think so?"

I pretended a confidence I didn't feel. "Absolutely."

She heaved a huge sigh, a smile lighting her face. "Tash, you've always been just the nicest person and you're one of the few folks here who doesn't treat me like the... the *help*." She leaned forward, dropping her voice to a whisper. "And if I hear anything about your job? I promise I'll let you know straightaway."

"Thanks, Alaia." I made a mental note to add her name to my handmade Christmas card list. "I really appreciate it. Forewarned is forearmed, right?"

I trudged back to my office and managed to get a little work done, although I was still distracted by yesterday's events, Alaia's concerns, and PJ's continued radio silence. Neal didn't contact me either. I caught sight of him rushing around in the distance a few times, although I was never able to get close enough to initiate a conversation. I was desperate enough to stop by the HR director's office just before lunch, but she wasn't there, and her desk was suspiciously clear.

I ate my leftovers, although I kept a fortune cookie for PJ. Then, in the middle of the afternoon, after an extremely frustrating conversation with a delinquent vendor, I looked up to find him sprawled in my guest chair. He had dark circles under his eyes, his shirt was rumpled, and his untied bow tie hung limp on his chest. His quiff, usually meticulously styled, was standing up like a rooster's comb.

"Peej? Are you okay?"

He peered at me from half-closed eyes. "Do I *look* okay?"

"No. You look like—"

"Don't say it. I prefer to imagine myself in my usual pristine condition." He lifted one end of his bow tie between his thumb and forefinger. "Despite all evidence to the contrary."

"Sustenance?" I held out the fortune cookie.

"You are a queen." He took it and ripped open the plastic wrapper, but with the cookie in both hands, he froze. "I'm afraid to look. At the rate things are going, the stupid fortune will probably prophesy the zombie apocalypse or a return to MS-DOS."

"Bad day in IT?"

"Ugh. The worst." He eyed the cookie. "Oh, what the heck." He broke it open, set the fortune aside unread, and stuffed half the cookie in his mouth. "I wish these weren't so dry," he said, somehow managing not to spew crumbs across my desk.

"Hold on." I hurried to the break room and inserted a crumpled dollar to get him a Dr. Pepper from the vending machine. Yes, I was being a coward. Now that I was facing him after what was clearly a rough night, I didn't want to lay my own worries on him. But he'd be hurt and indignant if I kept it from him and he found out later—which he would, because a dead body wasn't exactly something you could sweep under the table—*ewww*—especially since his cousin was involved.

I stopped in my headlong rush back to the office, the can of cold soda in my hand. *Del.* I might not be able to divulge much information for fear of angering Bae and Huber, but PJ at least needed to know that something had happened at his cousin's job site, something that might affect him adversely.

The memory of that GTO and its bearded driver leaving the scene haunted me again. But I pushed it aside and entered my office. I handed the can to PJ. "A mouthful of Dr. Pepper helps the fortune cookie go down."

He took it eagerly. "Did I say you were a queen? I was wrong. You are a goddess." He took a gulp and then slumped in the chair. "Sorry I didn't get back to you yesterday. Vinh had us on communications lockdown for the first phase of the V&S integration."

"Bad?"

"Let's put it this way. If he *hadn't* insisted on the lockdown, we'd have all called 9-1-1. After either falling on our own swords or stabbing Vinh with them simultaneously."

"Speaking of 9-1-1," we both said at once.

"You first," we said in another chorus.

"No, really," I said, because I still didn't want to broach the subject, not with PJ looking like ten miles of bad road.

"So." He drew out the word, then took another swig of Dr. Pepper. "I wasn't on total comm lockdown last night. Vinh gave us a fifteen-minute break around eight and I could have called you. But I didn't."

I weaved my fingers together and rested them in my lap. "PJ, just because we're besties doesn't mean you're required to jump every time I say frog."

His eyebrows bunched. "To my certain knowledge, you've never said *frog* to me at all. Except when we're discussing Tiana's ball gown."

I gave him a look. "Peej."

"Right, right." He took a deep breath. "I used my recess to call Forrest."

"Forrest?" I frowned. "My lawyer friend? That Forrest?"

He canted one eyebrow. "You have other friends named Forrest?" But when I opened my mouth, he held up one hand. "Don't answer. I'm sure you have half a dozen Forrest friends." He cocked his head to the side, momentarily deep in thought. "That makes you sound like Snow White. Only the one in the *Shrek 3*, with the tattoo and the attack Bambi."

"I don't have a tattoo."

"I note you don't deny the attack Bambi." He shook his head. "Never mind. Anyway, yes, I called Forrest the lawyer. For Del."

I winced. "Oh dear. Did they arrest him?"

PJ narrowed his eyes. "Have something you want to share with the class, LaTashia? Who is this *they* of whom you speak?"

"Well... Bae and Huber."

"How did you know that Bae and Huber had their eyes on Del?"

"Because..." I bared my teeth in a grimace. "I sort of..."

"LaTashia," he said, his voice laced with warning.

"Discovered the body?"

He stared at me for a good ten seconds, then downed half of his remaining soda. "Of course you did. Really, LaTashia. Isn't it enough that you know every *living* Washington County resident? You absolutely must draw the line at the dead."

CHAPTER ELEVEN

"You didn't answer my question. Did they arrest Del?"

He shook his head. "No. But he called and told me they were about to take him in for questioning, and I didn't think he should go in alone. I know from personal experience that being interrogated by Detective Hottie is the opposite of comfortable." He scrunched up his nose, making his glasses bounce. "My pants were decidedly too tight after less than two minutes."

I blinked. "Do you, er, think Del might have that same reaction?"

PJ snorted a laugh. "Good grief, no. He's at the opposite end of the Kinsey scale from me." He waggled his eyebrows. "Now if *you* had been asking the questions…"

Heat rushed up my throat. "Stop it."

"And since I couldn't very well go with him, even if Vinh hadn't had us all chained in the IT dungeon, Forrest seemed like the best option. I knew he had experience with local law enforcement, the jail, and the detectives."

"But doesn't lawyering up make Del look guilty? If he's innocent—"

"He is," PJ said through clenched teeth. "Del is the most stand-up guy I know, and always has been."

"Then why—"

"Kate. Burns," he spat, and picked up the tiny strip of paper with the fortune on it. "Kate. Burns."

"The reporter?"

"You know about her?"

"She was on the scene yesterday."

He twisted the unread fortune in his fingers. "Of course she was." He leaned forward. "Since clearly you know more about this than I do, why don't you fill me in?"

"I'm not sure how much I can say. You know how Bae and Huber feel about us discussing an investigation before they've released the name of the victim."

"Del already spilled the beans, so you don't have to worry that they'll come for you." He slid down in the chair until his head was resting on the back. "I know that the deceased is the building inspector with the bad taste in suits, the one Del had at least one run-in with."

"That's right. You were there on Monday. You saw the confrontation."

PJ nodded glumly. "It doesn't look great."

"People can argue without attacking one another."

"Obviously, otherwise I'd have assaulted Vinh with a staple gun long ago." He sighed. "I told you Del just moved back up here recently. His family moved down to Southern California when he was in high school, and he stayed there. Went to trade school. Started his business down there. But then came Kate Burns. Or rather Reggie Burns."

"I'm guessing he's a relation."

His expression darkened. "Her brother. He was a carpenter. Worked for a subcontractor that Del used for some of his jobs."

"'Was?'"

"He died. On the construction site. But he was there after hours, which was against the rules. Apparently, he was behind on a task and his supervisor—the sub, not Del, who was the general contractor—was on his case. Reggie had other problems, too. Substance abuse. Anger management issues. Impulse control. Since Del insisted that all the tools be locked up at the end of the workday, Reggie brought along his own tools, specifically a circular saw."

I winced. "I'm not liking where this is going."

"Yeah. It's not pretty. The fool rested a board on his leg to make a cut and got a little more than wood. He bled out. Del found him there when he arrived the following day."

"That's..." Ugh. Poor Reggie. Poor Del. "Was there an inquiry?"

He nodded. "Yes. They found drugs in Reggie's system, enough to classify him as legally impaired. He'd clearly come to the site against the rules and brought his own equipment. It was ruled an accidental death. But Kate didn't accept it." He twisted the fortune around one finger. "There's a video."

"A video?"

"Yeah. She ambushed Del at the site and started firing questions at him, the kind you can't really answer. You know, the old 'Have you stopped beating your grandmother?' type thing. You can't say yes, because that's admitting you *have* beaten your grandmother and you can't say no because that means you still are." He shook his head. "The whole thing made Del look like *he* was the one with anger management and impulse control issues. I mean, until I saw the video, I didn't even know Del *could* get mad."

"So he left town?"

"Eventually. He was cleared by Cal-OSHA. There were never any charges filed. But *Realty Reports* wields a lot of bullying power in the So Cal real estate world. No developers were willing to hire Del's company anymore because if they did, Burns and her online rag would go after them." He shrugged. "And not all of them could stand up to that much scrutiny, if you get my drift."

"And now there's another accident associated with one of Del's jobs."

"Yep. And somehow Burns is on the spot to catch it. Coincidence? I think not. Now she'll spin events to show Del in the worst possible light." He unwound the fortune. "The rest of the Burns family accepted the findings. They knew Reggie had his problems, and this was exactly like something he'd do. They didn't blame Del, certainly not more than he blamed himself." He sniffed. "He paid for the funeral, for pity's sake, but Kate can't let it go."

He smoothed the fortune on his knee and peered down at it. His gaze sharpened, and he gave a disgusted snort. "Figures." He slapped the fortune on my desk blotter.

Error 404: Fortune not found.

Either Tang Dynasty's fortune cookie vendor had a twisted geek sense of humor—something PJ and I could totally appreciate—or else they had serious quality control issues. On any other day, we'd have laughed, and PJ would've tacked it to the bulletin board in the IT bullpen. But not today. Today, the irony hit a little too close to the bone.

I shifted in my seat and smoothed my lemon-patterned skirt. The way PJ's knee was bouncing, he had to be remembering his own not-so-distant experience at the county jail. "Are you sure Del hasn't been arrested? Have you spoken to him since last night?"

He nodded morosely. "At about six this morning."

"Well, at least Vinh didn't keep you *all* night."

He rolled his eyes. "Are you kidding? If he had his way, we'd *still* be there. He's determined to get *all the things* done before he even knows what *all the things* are. But I told Vinh to stuff it and led a walk-out." He scrunched up his face. "More of a stumble-out, actually. None of us are college students anymore. We can't exist on nothing but caffeine and rebellion."

I chuckled a little half-heartedly. "I don't know. I can vouch for your close personal relationship with caffeine in all its forms, and you're doing pretty well on the rebellion front if you all challenged Vinh."

PJ shrugged, a wicked twinkle in his eyes. "I threatened him with HR. Vinh may be an obsessive workaholic with control issues, but he's an obsessive workaholic with control issues and a deep respect for rules."

"And Del?" I threaded my fingers together and squeezed. He wasn't going to like what I was about to say. "Peej, if he moved away in his teens, you haven't really known him for years. Is it possible he could have had something to do with Jenkins' death?"

That brought him upright. "Absolutely not. Just because we didn't live near one another didn't mean we didn't still see each other at family events. We may have drifted apart a little bit when our career paths diverged, me veering into engineering and him into construction, but we still spoke often. He was"—PJ's voice broke—"my best friend until he moved. We had each other's backs when we were kids, the same as you and I do now." He held out his arms. "And you know me, Tash. Who do you think was the pugnacious one in that duo? Pro tip: It wasn't Del."

"Okay, but—"

"He feels guilty when he swats *mosquitos*, for pity's sake. The only thing that ever got under his skin was when somebody was mean to me, or when somebody questioned his integrity or the quality of his work."

"Like Jenkins did," I said quietly. "I saw his reaction at the Airship Ambassador. So did Margaret. If Bae asks us, we'll have to tell him."

Behind his glasses, PJ's eyes turned pleading. "But he didn't *do* anything. You saw that too."

"That's right. I won't speculate or draw conclusions." Speculation was all I'd be doing if I brought up the GTO now. "But if Bae or Huber asks, I'll answer truthfully."

"I know. You're as bad as Del when it comes to personal ethics," he groused.

"Bad? Don't you mean *good*? And I might remind you that you're exactly the same."

His lips twitched as though he were trying not to smile. "I'll concede that. Provisionally."

"So you talked to Del. Is he okay?"

"Mostly." He leaned forward and picked up my favorite purple Lamy fountain pen. "Get this. Tillman had already called him before I did."

I blinked. "But you called him at six. Tillman called before that?"

"Yup, and fit to be tied because Detective Hottie refuses to let work resume on the bar until they've finished with the scene. Apparently, he was burning up the phone lines to the investigations department last night too. Since our friendly neighborhood detectives didn't give him any satisfaction, he started leaning on Del, threatening him with penalties if the work isn't completed on time."

"Can he do that?"

PJ grimaced. "Del's contract with Tillman includes penalties for every day beyond the deadline that the work's not complete."

"Why would he agree to something like that?"

"Hello? Because he didn't have a *choice*. He's trying to establish himself up here." He placed my fountain back on my desk, taking great care to position it perfectly parallel with the edge of my desk mat. "And then Kate Burns comes along to stir that nasty old pot. Somebody should bonk *her* on the head."

"Peej," I said with a glance at the open door, "maybe making random threats of violence where anybody could hear isn't the best strategy."

"Oh. Good point." He leaned over the chair arm and snagged the door's handle, swinging it closed. "There. *Now* can I make random threats of violence?"

I put my fingers in my ears. "La la la. Plausible deniability."

Just as I hoped, he laughed. "I'm clearly a very bad influence on you, LaTashia."

"No, dahhhling. You're the best."

He waved a hand in front of his face. "Oh stop. I'm weak enough from sleep deprivation that I'll cry at the drop of a sentimental hat."

My personal cell vibrated, rattling in the metal drawer I kept it in whenever I was at my desk. I slid the drawer open to check on the caller ID despite my no-personal-calls-at-work rule because, as PJ would say, *Hello?* Discovering another body, Del being involved, the Airship Ambassador being affected—this definitely wasn't business as usual.

I glanced from the phone to PJ. "It's Margaret."

He flapped his hands at me. "Well, answer it, for pity's sake. She's right there at the scene. Maybe she's heard something."

I forbore reminding him that even if she had heard something, if it was directly related to the investigation, she might not be able to share. But I answered it anyway. "Margaret? Is everything okay?"

"Oh, Tash," she said, her voice a little wobbly, "I need to—"

My office door burst open and Rhonda, my real estate agent, stepped inside, grinning widely, with her boxy sky blue linen jacket buttoned wrong and at least two pencils jammed in her strawberry blonde French twist. "Well?" she said breathlessly. "Are you ready?"

CHAPTER TWELVE

I blinked at her, my mouth agape, as Margaret paused mid-explanation. "Tash? Are you still there?"

"I'm sorry, Margaret. Can I call you back? I promise I won't be long."

"Okay." My heart sank at the uncertainty in her tone. Margaret was *never* anything less than confident. Something must really be wrong.

"Do you want me to stop by the tearoom?"

"Yes, please." The relief in her voice was obvious. "But call too."

"I will. I promise." I hung up and turned my attention to Rhonda, who was pressing a handful of her business cards on PJ. "Rhonda, how did you get in here?" Jensin Tech's security protocols were very specific—nobody got past the lobby without a visitor's pass and an escort from the person they were here to see. Rhonda wasn't sporting the green visitor's badge, and I hadn't gotten buzzed to let her in.

"Nobody was at the desk, and your office is listed right there on the directory, so I figured I'd just run on up."

"More to the point, why are you here?"

She widened her eyes behind her cat's-eye glasses. "We have an appointment. To see your *new house*." She beamed at us both. "Isn't it exciting?"

I heaved a sigh. Rhonda was good-hearted, but not the most organized person, despite the leather planner bristling with Post-it notes in her hand. "Our appointment isn't until tomorrow. And it's at five. Not three."

Her brow clouded. "Are you sure?" She flipped open the planner, sending a Post-it fluttering into PJ's lap. "I was certain — Aha!" She tapped the page. "Right here. The twelfth." She tilted the planner to one side. "Although I suppose that might be five. It's hard to keep inside these tiny lines."

"Rhonda. It's the eleventh."

She froze. "It is?"

PJ held up his phone with the date display front and center. "All day long."

Her smile returned, undiminished. "*That* must be why the seller was so confused when I called to confirm!" Her expression turned hopeful. "Could we go now, anyway? I mean, I'm here. You're here." She gestured with her planner, releasing another flock of Post-its. "He's here." She accepted the collected Post-its from PJ. "Who are you again?"

He shot me a sly sidelong glance. "Your worst nightmare," he said, in his best Michael Keaton-as-Batman voice.

She blinked at him. "I'm sorry. What?"

He stood up, brushing irritably at the wrinkles in his shirt. "I'm her best friend. She makes *zero* decisions without consulting with me. Let's go."

"Okay." She glanced from me to PJ, obviously not certain what to do—a frequent reaction to anybody who didn't know him.

"Are you sure, Peej? Wouldn't you rather go home and get some rest?"

"I've consumed far too much Red Bull to be able to sleep any time in the next millennium, and I'd rather get out of here before I get sucked back into Vinh's vortex of geek doom or hang about up here while people glance furtively around, wondering who they can throw under the bus so they don't get downsized."

"If you're sure." I couldn't deny I was relieved. PJ was right —I always consulted him on major life decisions. And given the latest drama—both workplace and suspicious death related—I could really use a distraction. As I gathered my purse, tucking work and personal phones inside, a little of the thrill I'd felt when Rhonda first sent me the links to the house returned. "Did you drive today?"

"You mean yesterday?" PJ said sourly. "No, thank goodness. I left Moocher safely at home and took MAX." PJ was devoted to his MINI Cooper, but given his exhaustion, I was glad he wouldn't be tempted to get behind the wheel. I'd have insisted on driving him home, anyway.

"You can ride with me. I've got the address—"

"Oh, no!" Rhonda said brightly. "You can both ride with me. That's the way we real estate agents do it. And there's plenty of room in my Kia."

PJ gestured for Rhonda and me to precede him. "Lead on. I'm more than willing to be chauffeured about town."

Nobody looked twice at us as we filed out of my office, PJ's snark about furtive glances notwithstanding. And since nobody was at the reception desk in the lobby either, nobody saw us march out to the parking lot. Rhonda led us to a rather dusty red Kia SUV, unlocking it with her fob.

PJ strode determinedly to the rear driver's side door. "You take shotgun, LaTashia. This is your rodeo, after all."

"Is that why you invited yourself along?" I teased as I circled the car.

"Please," he scoffed as he opened the door. "You know you couldn't do this without— Um, excuse me, Rhonda?"

"Yes?" she asked as she adjusted the rearview mirror.

"Why do you have a box of obviously nonfunctional cassette tapes in your back seat?"

"Oh, are they in the way?" She twisted around to look at him. "I can put them in the back if you want."

He smiled benignly at Rhonda. "No need. I've got plenty of room since I— Good grief." He stuck his hand in the box and pulled something out. "A five and a quarter inch floppy disk. I haven't seen one of these since I cleaned out my grandmother's attic." His eyes widened. "And is that an eight-track tape?"

Rhonda nodded as she started the car. "Yes. It took me a long time to find them. The zip drives too, although I didn't have too much trouble with the CDs."

"Rhonda," I said, mystified as PJ cooed over an old Gameboy cartridge. "Why do you have all that stuff?"

She beamed again as she pulled onto the street. "It's for you, Tash!"

My jaw dropped. "Me? Whatever— I mean, it's nice for you to think of me, but why would you..." I gestured helplessly.

"You told me the other day that you were planning some mixed media projects. So I sourced some mixed media for you." She reached over and patted my arm. "It seemed the least I could do for you, since you're helping me launch my new career."

I heard PJ choke on a laugh and very deliberately didn't look at him. "That's very... thoughtful of you." I cleared my throat. "Th-thank you." It was the thought that counted, right? She'd clearly gone to a lot of trouble, and if nothing else, PJ had a line on companies that recycled or safely disposed of old tech.

"You're certainly welcome." She launched into a spiel that started out extolling the virtues of the house we were about to view, but somehow ended up switching to the lack of decent coffee in her office. She pulled up next to Insomnia Coffee in downtown Hillsboro. "Do you mind? I'll just be a second."

"No worries. PJ and I—" But a soft snore from the back seat clued me in that PJ wouldn't be ready to chat. Sure enough, when I glanced back, he was out like a light, a PS2 game cartridge in his limp fingers. "I've got a call to make, anyway. Take your time."

As soon as she got out, I dialed Margaret. "Hey," I said softly. "You okay?"

"I'm doing as well as can be expected. Why are you whispering?"

"I'm on my way to look at a possible house with my real estate agent"—who had very little concept of craft terminology —"and PJ, who's asleep in the back seat of the agent's car."

"Oh." She sounded defeated. "So you won't be stopping by?"

"I most certainly will be stopping by. We both will. But it'll be after Rhonda shows us the house and takes us back to collect my car. What's up?"

"Well…" I could imagine her twisting a lock of hair that had fallen out of her bun around her finger. "Remember last night I left to track down Hank?"

"Yes."

"I couldn't. At least not for a couple of hours."

The skin along my spine prickled. "I'm sure he had a reason."

"Yes. But not a great one."

"Margaret—"

"Oh, he's usually hip deep in some project in his workshop, but that wasn't the case last night. So in terms of keeping him in the clear for the murder—"

"It's definitely a murder? Did the ME confirm it?"

"Yes. Oh. Wasn't I supposed to say that?"

I sighed. "Technically, no, not without the detectives' permission. But since I discovered the body, it's not exactly news to me." However, I'd been holding on to a slim hope that Jenkins' electrocution might be ruled an accident. "Did they establish a time of death?"

"They didn't tell me. But they were asking for our whereabouts all afternoon, right up until you made your 9-1-1 call."

I grimaced. What a day for the tea shop to be closed. If they'd been open for business, both Hank and Margaret would have had multiple witnesses. On the other hand, their customers didn't need the trauma of proximity to a crime scene, either.

"I was working on the restroom decor," Margaret continued. "I was able to finish up the mosaic with those coins PJ brought, but I was by myself."

I thought hard. "I took a picture of the unfinished mosaic on Monday, so I can prove you were working on it."

"Yes, but not what time. The thing is… Hank left around two. He called me at three from Tillman's office. He managed to confront Tillman about the building sale. He said it got… heated. Not that he did anything," she hurried to add. "But Hank is a big guy, and he's always got a ready-made blunt object with him because of his cane. Tillman ordered him out and said something about not threatening him and the sale was going through on time no matter what. Tillman's assistant and the other person in the reception area heard them. Heard Hank say he'd do what he could to block the sale."

Ugh. "That doesn't sound great, but it doesn't mean anything."

"Except the other person in the reception area was Donald Jenkins. And Tash?" Her voice faded to almost nothing. "They want Hank's walking stick. To test for blood."

"But why? Jenkins was electrocuted."

"No, he wasn't. The cause of death was… was…" My belly jolted when I remembered that telltale scent of blood, not common with electrocutions, and I knew what Margaret's next words would be. "… a catastrophic head wound. Inflicted by a heavy object made of wood."

CHAPTER THIRTEEN

I was still chewing over Margaret's revelation when Rhonda returned and set a bag redolent of coffee and another of freshly baked cookies on top of her box of "mixed media."

"All set!" she said brightly. She only drove a few blocks before pulling to an abrupt stop in front of a Craftsman-style bungalow in an established neighborhood just outside of downtown.

With a snort, PJ jerked awake, sending the game cartridge clattering to the floor mat. "Are we there yet?"

I peered through the window. There was a *For Sale* sign on the rather overgrown lawn with Rhonda's name and number on it. "This isn't my house."

"No. You don't mind, do you?" She reached back to snag the bag of cookies. "I'm staging it for another client. You can come in if you want." She jumped out and hurried up to the wide front porch.

PJ blinked owlishly. "She has another client?"

"Apparently, she has her own listing." I pointed to the sign.

"Heaven help them," he muttered as he opened his door. "Come on. If I stay here, I'll just fall asleep again." He leaned back into the car and murmured, "And I'm definitely stealing one of those cookies."

I frowned slightly as I climbed out and accompanied PJ up the sidewalk. Margaret's worries were affecting me. I was sure

Hank couldn't have anything to do with Jenkins' death, but PJ was sure Del couldn't either. I wanted a suspect that I didn't *like*, dang it!

Rhonda had left the front door ajar and even though this wasn't *my* house, I had to admit the door was nice. Well-kept, polished wood, its top rounded in an arch with a spoked fanlight at eye-level.

PJ tapped the beveled glass. "This looks like something that would fit right into the Airship Ambassador's decor. Maybe you should take notes for Margaret." But when he pushed the door open, we were met with a gold starburst linoleum entry that opened into a vast expanse of worn orange shag carpet. He clapped a hand over his eyes. "It burns! Never mind. Ugh. The seventies are calling, and they want their color scheme back."

"Shhh. Don't be such a drama queen."

He peeked at me through his fingers. "Really, LaTashia, it's like you don't even know me." He dropped his hands and prowled through the living room and into a dining room. "Aha!" He darted through another arched doorway.

I followed, looking at the empty rooms with a different perspective. I was about to view my first potential house. How likely was it that my first option would be my last? How many people would troop through this place before somebody decided it was perfect for them? I found PJ in the kitchen, brushing telltale cookie crumbs from his shirt. "Those weren't for us."

He gestured to the plate, which sat on the avocado green Formica counter next to a stack of flyers about the house. "I only took one." He quickly rearranged the remaining cookies. "Okay, two. But you can hardly tell." He sniffed experimentally. "Although I'm not sure even cookies could mask the unmistakable evidence that the previous owner kept a cat."

"Well, I suppose you would know now."

"Please." He stuck his nose in the air. "Mary Pickford is *extremely* fastidious. She wouldn't be caught dead peeing on orange shag."

"Whatever you say."

Rhonda bustled into the room. "Isn't this just the cutest? The last owner lived here for forty years."

PJ eyed the harvest gold refrigerator. "Imagine that."

She handed PJ and me each a few of the flyers. "It's my first listing. If you know anybody who's interested, I'd love it if you could spread the word."

"Of course." I stowed the flyers in my purse and glared at PJ over Rhonda's head when he tried to slip his back onto the pile. He rolled his eyes but folded the flyers and tucked them into his back pocket.

Rhonda clapped her hands. "Now, are you ready to see *your* house?"

My stomach fluttered and I bounced on my toes. "I can't wait."

We piled back into Rhonda's car. She kept up a line of chatter all the way to Tualatin, interspersing details on the house we were about to see with comments about the house we'd just left. I glanced back at PJ whose eyes were starting to glaze over.

But when we pulled up to *my* house, he frowned as he peered out the window. "This is it?"

"That's right!" Rhonda sang. "Just wait until you see Tash's new craft room." She popped out her door and headed up the short sidewalk to fuss with the lockbox.

I studied PJ's expression as he continued to stare at the house. He looked... unimpressed. One thing I'd learned about PJ over the years of our friendship: His opinion was *always* right there on his face. Now he could almost pass for one of those bland audio-animatronic dolls from *It's a Small World*. "Peej? What are you thinking?"

He took a deep breath. "I'll reserve judgment until we see what it's like inside."

I raised my eyebrows. "You *never* reserve judgment."

He huffed. "Fine. First impression? Ugh. It's a boring ranch-style house, and you know I've never been a fan of default mid-century style. That last orange-shagged travesty had more personality." He scanned the street. "And a better neighborhood."

My heart sank a little. I valued PJ's opinion, and it usually marched pretty well with my own. Rhonda was beckoning to us from the front stoop—this house didn't have a porch or even much of an overhang over the door. "Let's go inside. I really want you to see the craft room."

He gave me a knowing look. "Oh, I see how it is now. You're willing to forgo architectural charm, a prime location, and a porch to die for in favor of the perfect crafting cave. *So* predictable, LaTashia."

"Please, Peej?"

His gaze softened. "Anything for you, my darling." He reached through the seats and took my hand. "But please. Put that fabulous analytical brain of yours fully online and don't let yourself be swayed by one perfect feature. Look at everything and keep in mind that any room can be transformed into an acceptable crafting venue with a little elbow grease and a visit to Home Depot."

I nodded. "I'll try not to be an impulse buyer."

"Good. Because choosing a house is not like picking out a new wig to match our next cosplay adventure. For one thing, it costs one heck of a lot more. For another, this will be your *home*, Tash. Imagine yourself *living* here, not just crafting here."

"I promise."

"Then let's go."

But despite my promise, I found it hard to focus on anything else when faced with that glorious craft room. It was even bigger than it looked in the photos, and the view over the deep back lawn would be an inspiration regardless of the season. I ran my hands over the built-in shelves, peered into the walk-in closet, and pictured my projects arranged over the generous counter space. Two words: grand scale.

"Tash?" PJ called, his voice echoing down the hallway. "Isn't this kitchen a little dark and cramped?"

"Kitchen?" I opened a shallow drawer in the built-in armoire and couldn't hold back a little squee. It was fitted with wooden dividers, creating a couple dozen little cubbies perfect for storing embellishments.

"Yes." PJ appeared in the door. "You know. The place where you cook? Or in my case, store takeout?"

"I'm sure it'll be fine. Have you *seen* the storage in here? I'll have plenty of room for all Ava's supplies as well as my own. And that spot by the north-facing window is *perfect* for my easel."

He threw up his hands and stalked back down the hallway, muttering, "Location, location, location."

Rhonda rejoined me, casting a doubtful glance over her shoulder at PJ before turning to me, her planner clutched to her chest. "Well?"

I took a deep breath. "Let's do this. Make an offer." We'd already talked about my budget, and I'd been pre-approved for a loan. "Full asking price. I don't want to lose out on this." Because no matter what PJ said, my craft room would be the heart of my home, and I could almost feel this one beating around me already.

PJ didn't say much as Rhonda and I discussed the offer on the way back to the office. I glanced at him from time to time, but he was always either poking through the box of "mixed media" or studying the flyer from the Hillsboro house.

When we got to the parking lot outside Jensin Tech, it was already half empty—unsurprising since it was past five. Rhonda leaned across the console to give me an awkward hug. "I'll get back to you as soon as I hear anything from the listing agent. But congratulations, Tash. You're about to be a homeowner!"

We got out, PJ still not saying anything as we watched Rhonda drive off. I nudged him with one elbow. "Peej? Aren't you going to say anything?"

He sighed. "I'm happy if you're happy."

I glared at him. "That's not exactly a ringing endorsement."

"It doesn't matter, babycakes. It's *your* house. I'm sure I'll grace it with my presence, probably more often than you'd prefer—"

"You're *always* welcome!" I protested.

"I know. But bottom line? You're the one who'll be living there, so…" He shrugged. "If you're happy, I'm happy."

I wanted to push him a little more, because the butterflies dancing in my middle weren't quite sure if they were on Team Euphoria or Team Terror. But he was exhausted, so I decided to let it go for now. We could sort it out later. In the meantime—

"Margaret!"

"I know it's been a thrilling day for you, but I'm PJ, not Margaret."

"No, I mean I told Margaret I'd come by the tearoom. She's freaking out a little about the… you know."

"Oh, poor baby. Let's go then."

I eyed his rumpled clothing and red-rimmed eyes. "Are you sure you don't want me to drop you at home?"

He waved a negligent hand. "Not a chance. Our Margaret needs moral support, and I am *always* supportive, although not always moral. Besides"—he patted my arm—"there'll be scones. And I'm in need of far more sustenance than a single cookie."

My lips twitched. "Don't you mean two cookies?"

"Details."

CHAPTER FOURTEEN

A familiar Oregon autumn drizzle started to fall as we left the Jensin Tech lot. I glanced over at PJ who was still unnaturally silent, but he was frowning at his phone, a wrinkle between his brows that either denoted a headache—totally possible, given he'd had maybe ten minutes' sleep in the last thirty-six hours—or worry.

"Peej? Is everything okay?"

His phone pinged with an incoming text, and his frown deepened. "It would have a much greater likelihood of okayness if Vinh would give it a freaking rest." He leaned back against the headrest. "He's under the impression that his staff is composed of a combination of Terminators, Commander Datas, and Wall-Es." He sighed. "Somebody needs to remind him occasionally that we are neither cyborgs nor droids."

I waited for him to return the text, but he just stared at the screen. "I take it you're not planning to be the reminder in question?"

He rolled his head to peer at me, my intermittent windshield wipers casting occasional shadow stripes across his face. "I rallied round the flag earlier. Now I'm just pretending that he paid attention and doesn't expect me to respond until tomorrow."

I glanced sidelong at him as I turned a corner. "Is that the only thing that's worrying you?"

"Not really." The phone pinged again, and once more, PJ ignored it. Instead, he sighed and said, "It's Del."

My little guilt worm gave a wiggle in my belly. "What about him?"

"I haven't heard anything more from him."

"Do you think he might have been arrested after all?"

"What?" His eyes widened. "No. He left me a voicemail after he and Forrest met with the detectives, and they just wanted him to be available if they had more questions. Not likely he'll go anywhere, anyway. Tillman is still insisting he meet the original deadline, even though the police haven't cleared the scene yet." He scowled out of the speckled windshield. "And of course, freaking Kate Burns had to post an article today."

I nearly swerved but corrected quickly to keep us safely on the road. "About the murder? Did she accuse Del?"

"No. Not quite, anyway, since she'd be skating on thin slander ice. It's all about some kind of sketchy real estate-slash-insurance fraud conspiracy that nobody seems to know anything about except her. But she somehow managed to squeeze in a few juicy insinuations about Del's work ethics, since the job where her brother died ended up with a massive insurance payout."

"Why? I mean, if Del was cleared of all charges and it was ruled accidentally self-inflicted."

He sniffed. "Developer liability coverage. Of course, Kate freaking Burns doesn't mention *that*. She makes it sound like it was on Del's contractor's bond and E&O policy."

"Go ahead and call him now if it'll make you feel better."

"You don't mind?"

I gave him the side-eye. "Seriously, PJ? It's like you don't even know me."

He laughed at me parroting his earlier snark. "I love you to bits, LaTashia."

"Back atcha, kiddo."

But despite multiple attempts, Del didn't answer. PJ finally muttered something distinctly unflattering and tucked his phone away, although I think his expletive was directed at Vinh, who'd continued to text him.

The drizzle let up by the time we pulled into the parking lot in back of the Airship Ambassador. Dusk had fallen, and the clouds that had crowded in soon after we got back from *my* house made it darker. My headlights swung over the empty lot, gleaming on the wet asphalt except for a dry patch that marked where somebody must have recently left. Since I had my pick of parking spots, I chose one right next to a lamppost to take advantage of its barely adequate light.

After I switched off the car, PJ climbed out and glared at the pole. "You'd think the businesses around here would insist on better illumination. I know this is Beaverton and not the mean streets of gangland Chicago, but I'd think they'd be more concerned for their customers' safety and peace of mind."

"Preaching to the choir, my friend. Margaret and Hank feel the same, but it's the building owners who are responsible."

"Let me guess. Tillman, the world's skankiest landlord, is dragging his feet?"

"However did you guess?" I glanced at the dry rectangle and noticed a little puddle of oil. Del had said his GTO leaked oil. Had we just missed him? I glanced at PJ. He hadn't mentioned Del again after the failed attempt to contact him, but the worry wrinkle between his brows hadn't disappeared.

I clicked my key fob to lock my car, the flash of its headlights illuminating a pile of trash across the lot. "Honestly. The dumpster is *right there*. Would it have killed somebody to take the extra two steps?" I rounded my front bumper and headed toward the dumpster, only to have PJ step in front of me.

"LaTashia, why must I continually remind you? It is *not* your job to carry the can for everybody else in the universe. That is not your mess."

"I know. But weren't you just complaining about customer safety and peace of mind? Keeping the lot clear of refuse is important. It might attract"—I shuddered—"rats."

"Ugh! Don't even!"

"Look, if it's too icky, I'll leave it alone and have Margaret notify Tillman to get on whoever maintains the lot."

He blocked my way again. "Let somebody else clean up on aisle nine for a change. You—" He pointed at me. "Stay here and look decorative."

I chuckled. "Whatever you say. Although I'm not sure this skirt qualifies as decorative."

"Please. Every item in your entire wardrobe is a work of art. Now. Watch me work." He marched toward the dumpster and called over his shoulder, "Remember, I've had beaucoup practice lately with my many Free Geek safaris."

"I hardly think computer recycling is on the same level as scraping up garbage behind a restaurant."

"Pfft. Potayto, potahto. It's all the detritus of our scandalous consumer-centric society." He paused and turned back to me. "Maybe you should start converting things like this—or like that box of positively cobwebby tech that Rhonda gathered for you—into art."

"Trust me, I enjoy a found-object project as much as the next crafter, but I draw the line at organic waste."

"Fine. Be that way." He stalked toward the dumpster but stopped when he was about a foot away from the trash pile. He lifted up one foot. "Ewww. It's leaking. Who knows what kind of nastiness I'll have to clean off these shoes and they were already suffering from moving far too many server racks. They're scuffed, LaTashia. Scuffed. They may never recover and now I have garbage juice on them to boot." He lifted one foot with exaggerated care and took a giant step to the side. "Whoever tossed this is not only contributing to the burgeoning landfill, but to who knows what kind of toxic waste." He lifted the other foot. "If they..." He froze, teetering on one leg. "Tash?"

"Yes?"

He stared down at the bundle of rags. "There's a body."

CHAPTER FIFTEEN

My stomach flipped, and I had to take a few deep breaths to keep from hurling. "That's not funny, PJ."

He turned to me, his eyes wide. "Do I look like I'm laughing?" He stared at the ground, one foot still in the air. "This isn't garbage juice, is it?"

"Peej, stay where you are," I said as I pulled my phone out.

"Stay where I am?" he screeched, arms flailing as he tried to keep his balance. "LaTashia, I'm standing in *blood*. There is *blood* on my Ferragamos."

"Sweetie, what you're standing in is evidence." I dialed 9-1-1 for the second time in a week, trying to keep my roiling stomach under control.

"9-1-1. What's your emergency?"

"This is Tash Van Buren. I'm at—"

"Tash? This is Clarissa. We spoke the other day. Has something else happened at the construction site?"

Wonderful. Now I apparently had a personal 9-1-1 operator. "Yes. We're in the shared parking lot in back of the Magic Meatball restaurant and the Airship Ambassador tearoom." I gave her the address. "And we believe we've found another body."

"Help is on the way. Can you tell if the victim is breathing?"

"Um…" I glanced at PJ, who was still trying to keep his balance on one foot while keeping the other away from his jeans. "PJ? Can you tell if they're breathing?"

"You want me to *touch* it?" His glasses glinted in the uncertain light, but I knew from experience that when he used that tone of voice, his eyes were wide with terror.

"They're not an 'it,' Peej. They're a person, and the operator needs to know if they're breathing."

"Right." His voice was rough, raspy, nothing like his usual smooth tenor. "A person." He gingerly set his foot down and crouched over the body. "They're not moving at all. I can't detect any breath or—" He stood up so quickly he had to take a step backward to keep from falling over. "Tash. It's Kate Burns."

My stomach tumbled all the way to my yellow ballet flats. "Are you sure?"

He nodded. "Positive. She's on her stomach but I recognize her profile."

"She doesn't appear to be breathing," I told the operator. "And there's quite a pool of blood around her."

"The police are almost there. You can give them all the details, but please stay on the line with me until they arrive."

"Of course."

The sirens were audible now, from two directions. Police and EMTs, I guessed. We'd learned in our last rodeo with the Washington County first responders that law enforcement wasn't allowed to declare somebody dead—that determination had to come from a medical professional. The EMTs would probably contact the ME's office. Or something. My brain was whirling. That had to be the reason I was cataloging the steps in death scene processing.

I didn't want to think too hard about *why* I could catalogue the steps in death scene processing.

A police car pulled up in front of the entrance to the parking lot, effectively blocking it from any further traffic, and left its lights flashing. An ambulance pulled up behind them and the officers climbed out of their cruiser to confer while the EMTs hustled over to the body with their equipment.

"The police and the EMTs have arrived," I told the operator, "so I'll hang up now."

"Of course. Stay strong, Tash."

"Thanks, Clarissa. I'm really hoping this will be the last time you hear from me for..." I almost said "a while" but changed my mind at the last second. "...ever." Clarissa chuckled as I ended the call.

I tucked my phone away as the officers began taping off the parking lot. PJ grimaced at me. As an avid *Forensic Files* watcher, he'd been a little star-struck the first time he'd seen crime scene tape being deployed. I suspected the novelty had worn off by now.

He lifted a hand to greet the EMTs. "Is it all right if I move now? I, um, didn't want to disturb the scene too much."

One of the EMTs glanced down at PJ's feet. "Understood," she said as her partner hunkered down next to Kate's body. "Please remain where you are for the moment until the team arrives to process the scene. I'm sure they'll want your... footwear."

"Well, I certainly don't want it anymore," he muttered.

The second EMT stood up. "ME's on the way. There's nothing we can do for her."

It was official then—I'd discovered my fourth dead body. Although technically PJ had been the one to stumble on one of them, I'd been with him at the time.

A familiar dark sedan pulled up behind the police vehicle.

"Oh good grief," PJ moaned, "aren't there any other detectives in the whole freaking county? Why is it always *them*?"

Because of course it was Bae and Huber. They stepped onto the sidewalk as the ME's van arrived. The ME's team set up lights, illuminating the parking lot like a high school football field. It was bright enough that I could see PJ had turned decidedly green—probably because he could now see more crime scene details than he wanted.

One of the protective-suited team—I wasn't sure whether they were from the ME or a crime scene unit—escorted PJ over to where I was still standing by my car and held out an evidence bag. Resignedly, PJ toed off his shoes, hooked his fingers under the uppers, and dropped them into the bag.

He slumped against the CR-V's hatch, even though it was still dotted with the earlier drizzle. "You'd think I'd have learned by now *never* to wear any shoes I like when I go places with you. From now on, I'm wearing Walmart boat shoes *everywhere*."

I scooted next to him so our shoulders brushed. He was shivering. "Since you never set foot in Walmart, I'm finding that hard to believe."

"So I'll order online." He leaned against me. "How does this keep happening, Tash?" His voice was low and broken.

"I don't know, Peej. I really don't know."

Beyond Bae and Huber, who were standing on either side of the body like LEO bookends, one of the suited-up team turned Kate onto her back. Before our view of the body was blocked by the other responders, I saw it.

Protruding from her chest was a pair of very familiar rainbow rubber grips.

CHAPTER SIXTEEN

Bae and Huber hadn't kept us long. In fact, Bae had been so quick to finish questioning us that Huber had stared at him with her eyebrows raised as if he'd sprouted a second craggy, handsome head.

But they hadn't wanted us to go far. So, with a pot of tea in front of us—actually the second one, since PJ had downed the first one almost single-handedly after he'd spent twenty minutes in the restroom scrubbing his hands and feet—we were huddled with Margaret, watching the reflection of flashing red and blue lights in the windows of Assurance Insurance across the street.

Margaret was crumbling a scone onto her plate rather than actually eating any of it. "He said he was stuck in traffic."

I tore my gaze away from Assurance's grinning cartoon logo, still not able to decide if it was a raccoon or a squirrel, or why either of them made sense for an insurance company. "Who did?"

"Hank. On Wednesday. After he left Tillman's office."

"That's not unusual. Traffic out of downtown can be a bear at rush hour."

"But it's not exactly an airtight alibi, is it?" She pushed her plate of crumbs away.

"Margaret." I covered one of her hands with mine. "You can't possibly think Hank had anything to do with Jenkins' death."

"*I* don't. But what if he can't prove it? They gave his walking stick back—it was clean, of course—but a renovation must have lots of wood lying around and *anyone* could use a piece as a weapon, including Hank." She flipped her hand and gripped mine, almost painfully. "And today, he didn't come into the tearoom all day. He said he was in his workshop, but he didn't answer his phone when I called."

I tilted my head, puzzled. "Why should that matter?"

"Because," she said through clenched teeth, "getting rid of the inspector would be a great way to delay the building sale, not to mention there's been another murder in the same block."

"But the county must have other inspectors, and you and Hank didn't even know Kate. What earthly motive could he have to hurt either of them—assuming Hank could hurt anyone?"

She threw up her hands. "I don't know. But neither do the police. And innocent people can get convicted on circumstantial evidence all the time. There are dozens of episodes of *Forensic Files* about wrongful incarceration."

"Oooh." PJ's eyes went round over his seventh cup of tea. "You watch *Forensic Files* too? Did you see the one where the guy was in prison for, like, seventeen years before they found the evidence that cleared him?"

"Peej," I said, watching Margaret's face pale. "You're not helping."

PJ blinked. "Oh. Right. Sorry." Luckily, he got distracted because Bae strode into view in front of the plate-glass window, his khaki raincoat billowing behind him. He turned to face a stocky, mousey-haired man who, given his squint and untidy facial scruff, could've easily blended into an open call for smarmy henchmen. "Who's that man with Detective Hottie? He looks like he just ate a bushel of lemons with an Ex-Lax chaser."

"That," Margaret said, "is Jeffrey Tillman."

"*That's* Tillman?" PJ snagged a scone off the tray without looking. "I expected a wannabe property mogul to look more…

high-end, even in this town where millionaires traipse around in sandals with tube socks." He shuddered. "So wrong." He took a bite of the scone. "Mmm. Blueberry. Your scones can brighten the darkest night, Margaret, my dear."

Bae strode off back the way he'd come, and I didn't imagine it —PJ actually sighed. I shook my head. PJ's dating track record was nearly as disastrous as my own. The last thing he needed was to develop a crush on the detective who'd arrested him for murder.

Before Tillman could follow, Hank appeared outside, his face set determinedly and his cane striking the sidewalk with so much force we could hear the *thunk thunk thunk* at our table halfway back in the tearoom.

"Oh no," Margaret groaned. "Please tell me Hank isn't going to confront Tillman with the police literally ten feet from him."

But it looked like Hank was taking the high road. He nodded to Tillman curtly and would have passed by, but Tillman moved into his path.

"From that twitch in Hank's eye," PJ said around a mouthful of scone, "I'm guessing Tillman isn't offering to sell you the building at a really good price."

Margaret snorted. "You think?"

"He's probably trying to get Hank to join him in pushing the cops to clear the Rip Snorter crime scene so the renovations can proceed," PJ mused.

Margaret and I glanced at each other and then at PJ. "Tillman's pressuring the police?" she asked.

PJ tore his gaze from the increasingly animated conversation outside. "Yeah. Didn't you know?"

She shook her head. "Since when does Tillman share anything with us? He's been dodging us for weeks." Her expression darkened. "And now we know why."

I selected another scone, since PJ hadn't managed to eat them all nor Margaret to reduce them all to crumbs. "How do you know, Peej?"

"Del told me. Because Tillman's pressuring *him*." PJ's hand hovered over the last scone. "Dang. Now there's gonna be *another* delay since the parking lot's a crime scene too, isn't there? That means Tillman'll lean even harder on Del. Do you suppose they'll make you keep the tearoom closed longer?"

Margaret winced and then stood to gather the empty or crumb-filled plates. "I hope not. We're booked solid from next Wednesday on, and our margins are a lot narrower now that we have fewer tables on the floor." She gazed down at me, her expression halfway between hopeful and resigned. "Do you think they'll clear the scene soon, Tash?"

"Why would I know that?"

PJ scoffed. "Because you have four crime scenes under that very fetching belt."

"That doesn't mean I know how long these will take!"

"Hmmm. Good point." He drained his teacup. "They always try to be respectful of businesses, but with people dropping like flies all over Tillman's properties, they'll be more likely to take their time."

I exchanged a glance with Margaret. "Tillman doesn't own the parking lot himself, does he? I thought it was shared by the tearoom and the Magic Meatball."

"Oh, he owns the lot," Margaret tossed over her shoulder as she piled used plates on the counter by the kitchen door. "He makes us pay extra to let our customers park there, although apparently he didn't charge the Rip Snorter the same fee."

PJ nodded sagely. "From what I hear, he fancies himself a real estate tycoon. Although given the condition of the parking lot, he may not even rise to enlightened slum lord."

I narrowed my eyes at him. "How exactly did you hear this? You hadn't even heard of Tillman on Monday."

A faint pink blush infused his cheeks. "I, um, may have read Kate's article on him this afternoon." He held up his hands, palms out. "Only for research purposes." He glanced over his shoulder as if he expected somebody to pop out from behind the life-sized cardboard cut-out of H.G. Wells. "Don't tell Del."

Margaret rejoined us with a fresh plate of scones. "PJ's right. Tillman was involved in that development in Northeast a year or so ago. Remember? The one that went bust and was taken over by some big box warehouse chain to use for storage?"

"That was him?" It had been a big deal at the time because it was supposed to provide a mix of condos, restaurants, and high-end boutiques to revitalize the area. I'd been disappointed when it hadn't panned out because, from the sound of it, that kind of neighborhood would have been perfect for me.

"Partly him," Margaret said. "He had partners, which is one of the reasons he didn't go completely bankrupt. Of all the buildings he owns now, Airship Ambassador is the only lessee that's successful. I think he resents us and that's why he's been blowing us off."

Now that was a guy I could get behind as a murder suspect. Except he'd been a victim too, darn it. After all, it was his property that had been damaged, and his renovations that were suffering from the delays.

I hadn't had to point out the dry spot in the parking lot to the crime scene techs. They'd picked up on it right away, and I'd noticed them taking samples of the oil spill. Could they determine what car it came from forensically? Was that like ballistics or carpet fibers or fingerprints? I could hear PJ in my head: *"Good grief, LaTashia, are you suggesting they can test for* car DNA*?"*

Well, PJ's beloved *Forensic Files* proved they could identify a specific roll of duct tape or pair of sneakers. Why not oil from a specific vehicle? That car had left *after* Kate had been killed—I overheard one of the officers mention that the asphalt under her body had been dry, too.

Del's car wasn't the only one in the world with an oil leak. If they could identify the vehicle, it could just as easily exonerate him as convict him.

But what about the murder weapon? Yes, Del had a pair of those very distinctive needle-nosed pliers, but so did I. Dang it, I didn't want Del to be a killer. But even if he wasn't, if he'd just been in the wrong place at the wrong time, since PJ was the person who spent the most time with him, my bestie could be in danger, too. How could I convince him to keep his distance from Del without giving away my suspicions? Because if I was wrong and accused Del incorrectly, it might drive a wedge between PJ and me, and I didn't think I could handle that.

In the meantime, I'd figure out something, even if I had to convince Vinh to lock the IT staff up in frenzied merger prep for the foreseeable future.

CHAPTER SEVENTEEN

As though I'd conjured him, Del trudged into view outside. He paused when he saw Hank and Tillman having their—*ahem*—intense discussion and started to turn away, but Tillman beckoned him over rather peremptorily. Del didn't look too happy about joining the conversation, but he complied, nodding to Hank with a tight smile.

"Uh oh," PJ muttered. "This doesn't look good."

I studied the three of them—Hank, who could look me straight in the eye; Del, who topped me by several inches; and Tillman, who might not even match PJ's *medium* definition. That scene from *The Incredibles* popped into my head, the one where Bob Parr/Mr. Incredible gets dressed down by his insurance company boss who just barely reaches his waist. To anybody passing by, Tillman would look like the one at a disadvantage, but from the set of his chin and his wild gesticulations, he clearly believed he had the upper hand.

And since he was Hank's landlord and Del's employer, he probably did.

I winced when I remembered the outcome of that *Incredibles* scene—it had ended with the boss in traction after Bob launched him through several walls. Even a mild-mannered person could do damage if they were A) angry and B) disproportionately more physically powerful than their opponent.

I closed my eyes, trying to visualize Jenkins' size. He hadn't been as short as PJ, but he'd been shorter than Del, and significantly less broad across the chest. Del might have a little belly upholstery, but he had muscles too, muscles honed by physical labor rather than a gym, muscles somebody who spent their days behind a desk couldn't hope to match.

I opened my eyes again to find PJ biting his lip and staring at the scene outside. Del's face had lost any trace of affability. He looked just as teed off as when he'd been facing down Kate, and Hank didn't look much happier. Neither did Margaret, for that matter, although I suspected that her concern was tied more to her uncertainty over Hank's recent actions. *But maybe not.*

I cleared my throat. "Do you think they might get... physical with Tillman?"

PJ tore his gaze away from the apparently escalating argument. "Del? Not a chance. He's the kind of guy who carries spiders outside rather than step on them."

"Yeah, but spiders are actually useful," Margaret muttered.

"I wish we could hear what they're saying," PJ said with a pout. "How fair is it that we can witness the drama but can't listen to all the juicy details? It's like watching *Deadpool* with the sound turned off." His expression turned shifty. "Margaret, is the shade pulled down on the gift shop door?"

She nodded. "Yes. I didn't want a repeat of Monday when Jenkins barged in." She pressed her lips together into a grim line, probably remembering what had happened to Jenkins afterward.

"Excellent." PJ got up and crept away from the table toward the curtained doorway.

"Peej, what are you doing?" I whispered, although why I was bothering to lower my voice, I couldn't say. It wasn't like the men outside could hear us any more than we could hear them.

"Eavesdropping, of course. Don't ask silly questions, LaTashia." He slipped through the curtains into the gift shop.

I glanced sidelong at Margaret to find she was giving me the side-eye, too. "Well? Should we?" I asked.

Her answering grin, the slightly mischievous one that had been absent since Monday, warmed my heart. "Heck, yeah."

We hurried over to the curtain and peered through. PJ was crouched at the door, his ear pressed to the shade covering its glass. He was shielded from view by a display of stacked tea tins on one side and kitschy aprons on the other. He spotted us and beckoned us closer, so I sidled over to hide behind a hutch filled with tea sets while Margaret sheltered behind a rack of Doctor Who knitted scarves.

PJ held up a finger, his brow knotted as he pressed closer to the door. "I can't... They're not..." he murmured, then huffed an exasperated breath. "Honestly, these people have *no* consideration for eavesdroppers. They need to speak up!"

"Can you hear anything?" I whispered.

He waggled his hand back and forth, then his gaze landed on a row of *Alice in Wonderland* water glasses. He pointed to it and raised his eyebrows at Margaret, obviously asking permission. When she nodded, he grabbed a glass, set it against the door, and pressed his ear to it. "That's better."

I chewed on my lip, peering through a swoop in the hutch's curlicue trim at the men on the street. I could still see them from my angle, although Margaret, whose view out the window was blocked, and PJ, who was crouched behind the window shade, couldn't. While the argument didn't seem to be winding down, Tillman wasn't letting Hank or Del get a word in.

"Wow," PJ murmured. "Tillman is really a jerk."

"Tell me about it," Margaret grumbled.

"He's..." PJ squinted, as if that would help him hear better. "Complaining about the cops." He scowled. "Blaming Del that work can't continue."

"Why would he do that?" Margaret asked, and PJ shrugged.

"Now Tillman's giving it to Hank." PJ grimaced. "Ouch. Says he can sell his building whenever he wants, to whoever he wants." His eyes rounded. "Uh…"

"What? *What*?" Margaret whispered.

"He, um, hinted that the tearoom might not be around much longer."

Margaret paled. "He said that? The new owner plans to evict?"

"He said…" PJ stopped to listen again but shook his head. "More cop complaints. He said there might not be a place for the tearoom before long." He rolled his eyes. "Vaguespeak is *so* annoying."

I caught movement out of the corner of my eye. Tillman strode off down the street in the direction of the flashing lights. Hank said something to Del and then gestured to the tearoom. Del shook his head at first, but then nodded, his shoulders slumped, and the two men headed for the door.

"Hsst! They're coming!" I whispered.

PJ fumbled the Alice glass but managed to catch it before it fell and put it back on the display. Margaret whisked through the curtain into the main dining room and I'd made it to the arch when Hank's key grated in the lock, but as the door swung open, PJ was only halfway across the room.

He turned and gave them a rather manic smile. "Oh, hello there. We were just—"

"Spying?" Del said dryly.

PJ sniffed. "Really, Delbert, when have I ever done anything so mundane as *spy*?"

"Every chance you get?" Del stood aside as Hank relocked the door, although his gaze flickered to me before he focused on PJ again. "From when you were a kid, even before you read *Harriet the Spy*."

"I do not *spy*. Although I might admit to *reconnaissance*, but only under extreme duress." He shooed Hank and Del toward the curtain. "Go in, for pity's sake, and put us all out of our misery."

We all joined Margaret, who'd managed to install herself at one of the tables as though she'd never been lurking in the gift shop along with PJ and me. She even had a fresh tower of scones in front of her. I gave her serious props for that. The woman had mad skills.

She waited until we'd all taken our seats, then folded her hands on the table and said, "Well?"

Del stared at his empty plate, not even bothering with the scones. "I should never have taken this job."

With a huff, PJ lifted two scones onto Del's plate. "Why not? You have a right to make a living. You did nothing wrong." He bit into the orange marmalade scone he'd selected for himself.

Del picked up the ginger scone. Set it back down. "It was too soon. I should have known my reputation would follow me. I was sure as—" He glanced from me to Margaret. "As *heck* that Kate wasn't ready to let it go." His eyebrows drew together in a pained expression. "She loved her brother. I can respect that, even if she was misguided when it came to me. But she sure didn't deserve to die."

PJ had been about to take a bite of his scone, but he dropped it back on his plate with a soft *thunk*. "Kate. How did I forget?" He gazed at me plaintively. "LaTashia, please tell me I'm not getting hardened to finding dead bodies strewn across our path."

"Don't worry, Peej. I'm pretty sure nobody thinks you're hardened." I nudged his plate toward him. "And nobody will blame you for taking comfort where you can."

Hank took Margaret's hand. "Tillman hinted that—"

"The new owner might try to evict us?" Margaret nodded toward PJ. "We heard."

Hank's gaze turned steely. "He can try. But our lease specifies that any subsequent owner has to honor its terms, or the sale can't proceed. He's got no legal leg to stand on." He flicked his cane with a finger. "Even with a walking stick."

"Then why would he say something like that?" I asked, deliberately *not* looking at Del whose devastated expression wasn't anything I'd expect from a hardened killer. Of course, successful hardened killers probably needed to look properly remorseful, or they wouldn't be able to fly under law enforcement radar. "I mean, I get that Tillman's a tool, but what does he hope to accomplish?"

Hank shrugged. "Maybe it's just bravado. Maybe the new owner is insisting on a vacant building, and Tillman's hoping we'll decide to move on our own and save himself the lawsuit."

"But it's so stupid," Margaret said. "We'd have bought the building. He didn't need to go to somebody else at all."

"I don't think Tillman's that logical," Del said. "He seems like he's driven by ego and self-interest. Too bad I didn't know that before I took the job."

I frowned at him. "You didn't meet him beforehand?"

"No. It was a referral from my classic car repair group. A guy knew a guy who knew a guy who knew Tillman was looking for a GC. The classic car community isn't that big." Del sighed. "But I guess just because I share a hobby with somebody doesn't mean we share other values or activities."

I bit into my scone, hoping for PJ's sake that Del's values and activities didn't include homicidal mania and deadly force.

CHAPTER EIGHTEEN

The rest of the week at work hadn't gone any better for PJ or for me. I still hadn't managed to pin Neal down about my role in the newly merged company, and Vinh had his team working almost around the clock. PJ had invoked HR again, though, and IT was getting the weekend off.

On Saturday morning, I was working on a colorful mixed media collage, trying out some new techniques and using samples from a line of products a vendor had dropped off with their last delivery at Central Paper. Instead of working on the little gothic shadowboxes for the tearoom's gift shop, I'd tackled a bigger piece, one that was far more personal. The large canvas was coming together nicely as I incorporated ribbon and acrylic paint with magazine clippings I'd accumulated over the years.

The last week had really taken a toll on me. The high of making an offer on *my* house didn't offset the angst of the company merger or the horror of adding two to my accidentally discovered body count. At least this time Bae and Huber didn't seem to suspect me or PJ of being involved.

Did they suspect Del?

I'd finally called Huber and told her about the GTO I'd seen leaving the lot on Monday, and that the oil spot might be related, although I couldn't bring myself to mention Del's name. She'd thanked me and said they were already pursuing several leads.

I knew what that meant—*Keep your nose out of it, LaTashia.*

But I couldn't help remembering Del's gentleness as he'd handled Margaret's delicate china teacups, his shattered expression after Kate's body was discovered. Could he be that good an actor? But while faces could sometimes mislead, I had a thing about hands—all crafters do, to a certain extent, I think. And I couldn't make myself imagine those big, surprisingly deft hands lashing out with violence.

I sighed as I positioned my favorite image of Grace Jones on the piece. During some of my darkest moments, she was a pillar of strength who represented the ultimate in self-love, self-acceptance, and fierce individuality. Sometimes focusing on a project helped me clear my mind and led me to an epiphany about whatever was bothering me. So far today? No luck. Maybe because all the things on my mind—the house, the murders, the job—were too hopelessly tangled.

As I was selecting fragile dried rose petals from a ceramic bowl to place on the canvas, my work cell phone rang and the bowl wobbled in my grip, sending petals cascading to the floor. "Drat."

I glanced at the screen. *Neal.* I was tempted not to answer it—PJ and I had vowed to leave the office *at* the office all weekend—but I really needed to corner Neal about my job details. Given his success in dodging me all week, I couldn't miss the chance.

I grabbed the phone and answered the call. "Neal?"

"Heeeeyy, Tash. I'm glad I finally caught you."

I rolled my eyes. Seriously? "Well, you always know where to find me."

He cleared his throat. "Yes. Well." I could hear his fingers snapping and his fist slapping into his palm—he must have his headset on. "The thing is, we've got the merger."

"Yes, Neal. I was at the meeting." Not that I was paying very close attention.

"You always come through for me, Tash." He chuckled.

Okay, when Neal's chuckle was coupled with a statement about how I always gave in to his ridiculous demands, I could smell trouble coming. He hadn't technically asked a question yet, and since I didn't want to commit to anything, I waited.

It took him another couple of snap-slaps before he realized I wasn't going to say anything. "So. The merger. When I think of cooperation, I always think of you. I need someone to take point on the integration of our two major product lines. All the work you did last year on the detailed competitive comparisons for the sales team makes you the only person who is up to speed on both product offerings. I need you to liaise with their VP of product management and development. What do you say?"

"You mean you want me to work closely with the guy who, until very recently, you called The Joker because you considered him to be our most formidable nemesis? That guy?"

"Well… uh… yes."

I would have preferred saying nothing, because even if I said a flat no, somehow Neal would construe it as enthusiastic agreement. Instead, I took a deep breath. "Neal. What will my role be in the merged company?"

"Don't you worry about that, Tash. We can work all that out once all the T's are crossed and I's dotted."

"I'd really prefer a more solid—"

"Sorry, Tash. Got a call coming in from the V&S head honcho. I'm glad we've had this chat. I'll let him know that you're fully on board. Ciao."

I tossed the phone onto my cluttered workspace, barely missing the acrylic matte medium I was using to secure ephemera to my canvas. "Ugh." Why was I working for a dysfunctional boss who signed off a call with *ciao* non-ironically? Why did my belly knot whenever I thought about facing this Frankenstein mashup of two former competitors? Where had my joy in my work gone?

I sighed as I kneeled to collect the fallen rose petals. I knew where my joy had gone. Straight into my crafts. If only crafts paid the bills, I'd leave Jensin Tech in a heartbeat. From my spot on the floor, the sepia photo of my childhood home was directly at eye level. I stood quickly because it only reminded me of how loudly my father would object to me leaving a steady job in the industry, claiming that I was wasting my education. But I used my mechanical engineering training all the time when I designed a particularly complex craft project. If only I could leverage my MBA smarts to figure out how to make a living doing what I loved.

Oh, well. I sprayed some pale pink and clementine orange alcohol inks onto my canvas and used a sponge to blot the runoff. I could always decompress with my art. And no matter how toxic the work environment was, at least PJ was there to commiserate with me.

I checked my watch. Nearly two. I hadn't called PJ today, wanting him to catch up on sleep after Vinh's series of IT all-nighters. However, he'd have to get up soon. While he and I had been struggling at work, Margaret had been channeling her own stress into finishing the decor in the new restroom, and PJ and I were headed to the tearoom at four today for what he insisted on calling the Great Restroom Unveiling.

Margaret and Hank hadn't gotten the okay to reopen from the police yet, but she said Huber had promised her it wouldn't be much longer. So for now, we were all pretending like the Airship Ambassador could open as planned on Wednesday.

I glanced at the half dozen shadowboxes I'd completed so far. Two featured a blood-red, anatomically correct heart floating against my blackest black. Another box featured a mini Addams Family home with a tiny cemetery on a stormy night. The others featured ravens and a fake black widow spider who spelled "I love you" with her web.

I didn't want to overload Margaret with stock until we knew whether they'd sell, but I didn't want to short her either. The more I studied the finished boxes, the more I liked them—and the more they called out for another themed tea around

Halloween. So far, the tearoom had one in the winter, one in spring, and one in the summer. I bet an autumn event would be just as successful if it was positioned right.

A knock sounded at my door, followed by the key scraping in the lock. "Hellooo," PJ called. "I come bearing gifts."

I chuckled as I wiped ink off my hands with a soft rag and threaded my way through the boxes stacked in my craft room. He and I had keys to one another's apartments and cars, something that had come in handy more than once, but we always made a point to knock and announce ourselves, even when we were expected.

"What kind of gift—good heavens! What on earth are you doing with those?"

PJ stopped at the head of the stairs that led down to my garage and front door. He held the box of "mixed media" that Rhonda had thoughtfully—if not very accurately—collected for me. "I ran into Rhonda outside. She was so apologetic that she couldn't stop and chat, but she was heading over to present your offer to the homeowners, although why she couldn't have done that electronically in the first place, I have no idea. Maybe you're purchasing that boring ranch-style house from a nest of Luddites."

Well, that explained why Rhonda hadn't blown up my phone with news. She hadn't completed one of the most basic functions of her job. Perhaps Hank and Margaret were right about her lack of experience. What if I missed out on that glorious craft room because she was so slow to act? I rested my hand on one of the many supply-filled boxes and gave myself a mental shake. I couldn't completely blame Rhonda. I'd been so distracted by the news at work and... well... murder, that I hadn't followed up with her. *Everything will work out just fine, as long as we keep a positive attitude.*

"Peej," I said. "Don't dis my new home. You'll insult her, and then she might not welcome you."

He shuddered. "Ugh. I've seen more movies with hostile houses than I care to count, thank you so much for putting that in my head." He patted the side of the box. "Rhonda was mystified about why you forgot to take this with you the other day. I bore up manfully and didn't offer the obvious response."

I sighed as he set the box on my oak dining table. "Just what I need. More boxes."

"Don't worry, my darling. I'll take this lot with me and foist it onto Free Geek in my next inevitable run." He rolled his eyes. "Because now apparently we're not only clearing Jensin Tech's obsolete tech, we're ferrying V&S's moldy oldies, too." He flopped onto my sofa. "I didn't think anything would rival the mountain of CRTs, dot matrix printers, and 9600 baud modems that have been lurking in the Jensin's IT bowels since before the turn of the century, but V&S may have them beat." He slid down and rested his head on the rear cushion. "Although I'm not willing to conduct a hand recount to find out."

"So you hauled this box up the stairs as part of your exercise regimen? Why not stow it in Moocher right away?"

He didn't meet my gaze. "I, um…"

"Yes?"

"Oh fine. I didn't want to hurt Rhonda's feelings. She was so proud of finding all that stuff for you, and to tell you the truth, I'm low-key impressed at what she managed to dig up." He shifted his gaze from the corner and finally met my eyes. "But that doesn't mean that you should have to deal with it."

I smiled at him, my throat a little tight. He'd stepped in to prevent me from having to clear up the parking lot trash— which had turned out to be something else altogether—but he'd never uttered a single word of reproach. "Always looking out for me?"

"You know it, babycakes. It's you and me against the forces of… of…"

"Of conspicuous consumption?"

"I suppose we can't say evil in this case. But whatever." He pushed himself off the sofa. "But I brought more than recycling fodder." He edged past another stack of craft supplies and flipped open the flaps on Rhonda's box. "Subway!" He handed me a bag with a sandwich and a bag of chips. "As much as I adore Margaret's scones, a person can't live by scrumptious baked goods alone. And I guessed that if you were deep into the throes of crafting, you wouldn't have stopped for lunch."

He wasn't wrong. My stomach rumbled at the aroma of a turkey bacon melt with chipotle mayo. "Thank you, dahhhling. You're the best."

"I know," he said placidly, pulling out his own sandwich.

I grabbed plates and glasses the cupboard and passed one of each to him before retrieving the pitcher of filtered water from my fridge. I filled both our glasses. "Did you get some rest?" He looked marginally better, but still a little rough around the edges.

He took a sip of his water. "I'd have gotten more if Mary Pickford hadn't decided to challenge a sunbeam to a duel to the death."

"I'm surprised Kitty Kitty Paw Paw hasn't found a home for her yet. It's been more than three months now."

He poked at an errant lettuce leaf hanging out of his Italian B.M.T. "Nobody suitable has stepped up."

"Peej," I said, hiding my smile. "When are you going to admit that you're keeping her?"

CHAPTER NINETEEN

His look of mock outrage was so dramatic it would put the entire *Real Housewives* franchise to shame. "I'm not *keeping her.* Keeping a cat you're fostering is a fostering *fail,* and I do *not* fail."

"Mmhmmm. Whatever you say."

He narrowed his eyes. "That exceedingly smug tone does not become you, LaTashia."

I set my sandwich down. "All kidding aside, I'm just glad you have someone to keep you company, even if she's covered in fur and makes me sneeze. I mean, I've got my crafts to take my mind off... things. But you—"

"Have a boss who's more than happy to keep me busy 24/7." A smile curved his lips. "Although I do have to admit that coming home to a not-quite-empty apartment is... nice."

"There, see? That wasn't so hard, was it?"

"Only marginally painful." He opened his nacho cheese Doritos, which he claimed were one of any self-respecting geek's major food groups. "What vastly impressive project are you working on to keep your mind occupied?"

"Come and see." I pointed at a wad of Subway napkins next to him. "But maybe leave the Dorito dust behind."

"Please. What do you take me for? I know the proper respect to pay your artwork, even if I choose not to indulge in it myself." He stalked to the kitchen and washed his hands. "Now, lead the way."

I left my own sandwich behind because I didn't bring food or open drinks anywhere near my craft room and navigated the obstacle course my apartment had become since I'd inherited all of Ava's supplies.

A *thunk* sounded behind me. "Ow! It's a good thing you're plunging ahead into home ownership, LaTashia, because my shins won't survive this labyrinth of doom much longer."

A little thrill buzzed through me. *My house!* PJ was right, though—things couldn't remain the way they were. I led him to my canvas. "This."

PJ approached slowly until he stood next to me. He didn't say anything and didn't say anything and didn't say anything until I started to get nervous.

"Peej?"

He turned to me, and I was surprised to see his eyes swimming behind his glasses. Then he hugged me tight and gave a little sniff. "It's you. Every line. Every image. Every random piece of ribbon. It's all you."

I blinked rapidly, my own eyes prickling. Trust PJ to get what I was trying to do right out of the gate. "Yes."

He kissed my cheek and pulled away, brushing one hand under his eyes. "This is extraordinary, Tash. What are your plans for it?"

"I thought I'd hang it at the head of the stairs."

His eyes widened, nostrils flaring. "Absolutely not."

"You think there's a better place?"

"I'm not saying you can't hang it there *eventually*, but you need to share it too. Other people need to see it." He glanced around the crowded room, his gaze landing on a stack of magazines. He maneuvered his way around the boxes and sorted through the stack. He pulled one out. "Aha! This is the one."

I blinked at him. "You remember a specific craft magazine?"

"I became close, close personal friends with this one the day you bought it because you got sidetracked on our way out of Central Paper by some random customer who needed help with designing their wedding invitation."

I winced. "Sorry?"

"Water over the barrel," he said, rather inaccurately, waving one hand airily. "The point is"—he rifled through the magazine and jabbed a page with one finger—"this."

I peered at the article. "That's nothing like my project."

"I know, LaTashia, and that's the *point*. This rag accepts submissions by craftspeople and artisans, featuring them here, in full, glorious color, and accompanied by an article about the piece and about the *artist*." He shook the magazine, making the pages flutter. "Exposure, LaTashia. Social proof of your awesomeness. Something you'll need if you ever shake the dust of corporate America off your Chucks."

I stared at him, my heart in my throat. Could I? Goodness knows I wasn't exactly shy about my work, but I'd only shared it with friends, or locally with students in my classes, or at the tearoom gift shop. I'd never considered submitting something to a national magazine. "Do you really think I have a chance?"

"Honey-girl, you are a slam-dunk. Not only is your artwork superlative, but you can write, too." He turned to gaze at the project again. "I can tell just by looking at the unfinished piece that there are *stories* here, important stories about your experience that could have a huge impact on other people."

"I'm not exactly a guru, Peej."

He scoffed. "I'm not talking about starting your own religion, for pity's sake. But I think a lot of people—especially young Black women—would understand and benefit from being *seen*. Just like this. You're showing *yourself* here, joy and success, despite hardship and heartbreak. It's brilliant, Tash. Your work needs to be seen by the world."

"Thanks, Peej," I croaked. "That means a lot."

He smiled at me fondly and patted my shoulder. "You're a rockstar, my darling. It's my job as your roadie-slash-manager to make sure everybody knows it." He closed the magazine and set it back on the stack. "In fact, I may encourage Del to submit something too, even though I'd probably have to write the article for him. Those puzzle boxes of his would be perfect for the woodworking section. Did I ever show one to you?" He dug his phone out of his pocket and scrolled through his photos. "Look at this!"

"It's lovely." It really was, but I tried not to wince anyway. "PJ. About Del…"

He grinned at me as he tucked his phone away. "I *knew* there was a spark there! It was totally obvious on his side. I mean, he practically tripped over his own feet when he met you. And by the way, he's been hinting about wanting to meet you for *years*, since you've been a major part of my conversation whenever I've seen him. But I wasn't sure whether you were interested. You sly thing, you kept me guessing for long enough."

"PJ—"

"I need to set up a dinner party. You and Del." He scrunched up his face. "Shoot. I don't have a glimmer of a prospect at the moment. Nobody who's good enough to introduce to the two most important people in my life."

"That's not—"

"What about next Saturday? Or maybe tomorrow." He winked. "Now that I know the attraction isn't one-sided, why wait? I could throw together my famous lasagna." Another grimace. "No, bad choice. We don't want a garlic overload on a first date, now do we?"

"I really don't think—"

"Ooohhh." He nodded sagely. "You'd probably rather spend time alone with him. I shouldn't insert myself into this relationship already. Would you rather I keep out of your personal life?"

I heaved a sigh. "You know I'm fine with you up in my personal business, but—"

"Oh, thank heavens. Because I don't know how I could have *resisted*." He clasped his hands under his chin. "It's like a dream come true. I've always said we just need to find two good men —one for you and one for me—and we'd be set. And Del is definitely good." He scrunched his nose. "Way better than that *Bjorn*. Six-pack abs aren't *everything*." He winked again. "Although I personally wouldn't object when we get to work finding *my* good man, it's not a deal-breaker for me either."

"Please don't—"

"Bring Bjorn into the conversation?" He patted my arm. "Say no more, my darling. His name shall never again pass my lips, because now you'll have Del. I'm thinking maybe a nice pasta salad? Or—I've got it! Roast Cornish game hens! I've got a recipe to die for. Although—"

"PJ!" I shouted, which finally stopped his excited babble. "I don't want to date Del."

He blinked at me, his mouth agape. "You don't? Why not? If you gave him a chance, I'm sure—"

"That's not what—" I rubbed my hand over my face. "I mean, I didn't broach the subject because I want to date him."

His shoulder slumped in relief. "Oh, thank goodness. So dating him is still on the table? In that case, so are the roasted Cornish game hens. Tomorrow!" he crowed, thrusting a fist into the air in victory. "But I still won't have a viable date. Do you mind if it's just the three of us? That way, there won't be quite as much pressure on you while you *decide* to date him. I picked up an oil pump for him, so I can issue the invitation when I drop it off."

"PJ, the reason I brought Del up..." I gestured toward the living room. "Maybe we should go sit down?"

PJ froze. "Why do we need to sit?" He let his arm fall to his side. "I'm not sitting unless I know *why* I need to sit."

"Well... Why does Del need the oil pump?"

He frowned. "Because of the GTO's leak. He mentioned that to you the first day."

"Yes. I remember." I shifted my weight from one foot to the other. "Did you notice when we found Kate that there was a dry spot in the parking lot, as if somebody had left after the drizzle let up?"

"I was a little preoccupied with the blood on my Ferragamos. So no. I didn't."

"Well, it was there. And there was a... What looked like a fresh puddle of oil there too."

PJ stared at me. "What are you saying?" His voice had lost its usual snarky edge.

"I'm saying..." I took a deep breath. "I'm saying that Del's car leaks oil and there was clearly a car—a large one, longer than my CR-V—that had been parked in the lot around the time Kate was killed. And that the car leaked oil."

"That doesn't mean anything." PJ huffed, but his gaze slid away from mine. "Lots of cars leak oil. Besides, Del won't drive a leaky car. He hasn't driven the Goat for months because of it. He even had it shipped up from California."

"Are you sure he doesn't drive it? That he hasn't driven it? At all?"

PJ shook his head a little wildly. "He says it's bad for the environment. For pity's sake, LaTashia, that's why I'm bringing him the freaking oil pump!"

"Why couldn't he get it himself?"

"Because he finally got the call from Bae this morning. They cleared both the bar and the parking lot, and with Tillman hanging the penalty over his head, Del wanted to get right back on it, even if his subcontractors won't be on site until Monday. He asked me to meet his supplier..." He threw up his hands. "Oh good grief, it sounds like a freaking drug deal, not a delivery from a custom car parts shop."

"That's not all. The night I found Jenkins, I saw a GTO leaving the lot just as I arrived. Where does he disappear to?

Why is it that he's always just leaving but never there when the bodies are discovered?"

"*Millions* of people aren't there when the bodies are discovered," he said heatedly. "You'd be better off asking why *we're* always there when the bodies are discovered, because frankly, LaTashia, this is getting old."

"Peej, I saw the murder weapon that killed Kate. It was a pair of needle-nosed pliers. With rainbow rubber grips."

He stared at me stonily, his throat working, before shaking his head. "No. Del would never hurt anyone, any more than you would. I'd stake my life on it, and I refuse to argue with you about it anymore." He stood up. "Come on. We've got a bathroom unveiling to attend."

CHAPTER TWENTY

PJ didn't say much all the way to the tearoom. I kept glancing at him from the corner of my eye as I drove but didn't try to initiate any conversation. His body language—arms crossed, shoulders angled toward the door rather than toward me, his gaze focused out the window—practically shouted *Leave me alone*.

I hated this. *Hated* it. PJ had been a constant in my life since the day we'd met. Granted, eight years may not seem like a huge percentage in the scope of my nearly forty years, but PJ and his big personality and bigger heart took up a *lot* of space.

With only a few blocks left, I finally decided I couldn't let this stand. We *never* argued. Or rather, our arguments were about silly things, and usually more for amusement than actual disagreement. This felt different, because Del was clearly important to him, maybe more important than me. I didn't want to imagine what my life might be like if this caused a break between us, if PJ chose Del over me.

But just as disheartening was the idea that somebody PJ obviously loved could be a cold-blooded killer. Dang it, I'd *liked* Del. For that matter, I still did, deep down. PJ's nervous blathering about a potential date had, if I wanted to be honest with myself, planted a little seed of hope and excitement.

If *Del* found out I suspected him of murder, that would probably kill any chance of a future relationship, even if he *wasn't* a cold-blooded killer.

"Peej?" I said, my voice small. "I don't want to fight with you."

His shoulders sagged, but he continued to stare out the window. "Same."

"Can we put this aside for the time being? Time enough to deal with it when the police catch the killer."

"Whom you think is Del."

"I don't want to think it's him, for your sake as well as his. But you've got to admit that things don't look great for him."

"Well, things didn't look great for me last summer either, if you recall. Just because certain alleged evidence seems to point to a particular person doesn't make that particular person guilty."

I inclined my head. "Agreed. So truce?"

"I ought to say no, but I can't stay mad at you. And if…" He gripped his knees, knuckles whitening. "…if Del *is* involved, I'll need you more than ever."

"You've got me. You know that."

"Same."

So my heart was lighter as I took the last turn into the parking lot, although it sank a little when I saw that same gold GTO parked between a white Prius and a dusty blue Ford F150 pickup.

PJ huffed. "Well, Del's here this time and so are we, so let's hope the combination means we won't find any bodies today."

I was tempted to ask him how Del's car could be there when PJ swore that *Del* claimed he didn't drive it, but instead I just murmured "Amen," as I parked my car on the opposite side of the lot.

PJ hopped out and collected the oil pump in its plain white box from the back seat. He stomped across the lot, the box tucked under one arm, as he fished his keys out of his vintage barn jacket pocket. Apparently, I wasn't the only person who traded keys with PJ.

But instead of the GTO, he opened the pickup's door and set the oil pump inside.

"Why didn't you put that in Del's car?"

He closed the pickup's door with a solid thunk. "I did."

"But… Isn't that GTO his?"

"No. He's got a red ragtop."

My blood felt like it had been replaced with ice water. I was right, I was sure of it—that GTO belonged to the murderer. But the murderer wasn't Del.

However, the murderer could be *with* Del right this moment, upping their body count by one.

I sprinted for the sidewalk. "PJ, call Detective Bae. Now."

CHAPTER TWENTY-ONE

I thanked heaven that I'd worn my black and white Chucks instead of any of my kitten-heeled mules as I raced around the corner of the Magic Meatball with PJ at my side. He had his cell phone in his hand.

"What am I supposed to tell him?"

"Tell him… Tell him that the killer may be about to strike again."

"*What*?" PJ screeched. "Are you saying Del is—"

"No, I'm not." I stopped outside the Rip Snorter. The door was closed, but I hoped that whoever the perpetrator was, they hadn't gotten any smarter since their last attack and had left it unlocked. "I'm afraid the killer is about to strike *at* Del."

PJ's jaw tightened, his eyes narrowing behind his glasses. "Not on my— *our* watch." He punched in a number—I vaguely registered that it was a speed dial number—and barked, "Detective Bae? PJ Purdy."

I crept toward the door as he held a very clipped conversation with Bae. Maybe we'd gotten here in time. Maybe our presence would stop the killer. A tiny—probably far more logical—part of my brain whispered that with two or possibly three kills already under his belt, the murderer might not balk at adding two more. But if we could protect Del, somehow divert the killer's attention until the police arrived, I was willing to take the risk.

With my pepper spray in one hand, I tried the handle. *Unlocked.* My sigh of relief got ambushed by a nervous inhale as I eased the door open. I peered into the vestibule. Empty.

"Tash, Bae said—"

I turned my head, laying my finger over my lips, and PJ clamped his mouth shut and nodded. I waited, listening for any sound inside. Silence—but then a *thump* and a muffled curse. I could hear sirens approaching in the distance, and since I didn't want the noise to filter into the bar and alert the killer, I slipped inside, PJ right behind me.

I paused a moment to take a deep breath to settle my nerves, but nearly broke into a coughing fit. I managed to choke it back, but by the way PJ's nose was wrinkling, I knew he could smell it too. *Turpentine.* I'd done enough projects with oil-based paints to recognize the odor, and also to realize what a hazard it was not only for fire danger, but for fume inhalation.

Somehow, I suspected that whoever was spreading turps in the Rip Snorter wasn't concerned with ventilation. No, they intended to burn the place down. And if this place went up in flames, there was no way the Airship Ambassador—or Margaret and Hank waiting for us inside—would be spared.

I tiptoed across the vestibule to peek into the bar and had to stifle a yelp as I nearly tripped over a box the same shade as the flooring. The neat job site I remembered from last time I was here was now a shambles—the table saw toppled onto its side, wood scattered and broken, and tools and hardware flung everywhere. But that wasn't the most alarming thing.

There, amid the wood scraps and nails, lay Del, face down, not moving, with an incongruous gaily wrapped package next to his hand. I was torn between rushing over to see if he was still breathing, worried that whoever had attacked him would try again, and keeping PJ from seeing his cousin stretched out like way too many other victims we'd witnessed recently.

Then I saw Del's fingers twitch. *Still alive!* At least for now. But another thump sounded from somewhere down the hall.

The attacker was definitely still here. I clutched PJ's arm. "Call 9-1-1," I whispered.

His eyes widened. "Why?"

He'd have to give them details. I grabbed his arm and pulled him far enough over that he could see Del. He whimpered and started forward, but I kept my hold on him. "The best thing you can do for him is get the ambulance on the way. Tell them he's breathing."

"He is?" PJ's whisper was edged with hope.

"Yes. Just get them here." I pushed him toward the door. "From outside."

"But—"

"Just *do* it, PJ. And tell them there may be a fire hazard too. Warn Margaret and Hank."

If it had been anyone other than Del at risk, PJ probably would have argued with me. But he nodded curtly and slipped outside. I waited until the door closed behind him and then peeked into the bar again. Still no sign of the attacker. I didn't want to think what they might be up to, but the turpentine smell was definitely getting stronger. I needed to get Del out of here—for that matter, *I* really needed to get out of here—before the attacker lit a match.

Keeping one ear open for more sounds from the back room, I crept across the bar, sidestepping an upended box of screws, until I reached Del. To check his pulse, I moved the package aside, noting that it was solid and square, but not exceptionally heavy. At the base of Del's skull, a bloody lump was visible amid his thick, sandy hair. I winced. Blunt force trauma to the head was *never* a good thing.

I managed to locate a pulse... I thought. I'd taken the required CPR classes at work, but emergency medical care wasn't my forte. I glanced behind me. Still no movement from down the hall. I leaned forward. "Del?" I murmured. "Del, can you hear me?"

His fingers twitched and he moaned, so I took that as a positive sign.

"Just lie still. Help is on the way. You don't need to worry—"

"Who the hell are you?"

At the sound of the angry voice, I stood up so quickly I nearly overbalanced. When I turned, I had to stifle a gasp.

Jeffrey Tillman stood between me and the vestibule, a gallon can of turpentine in his hand. He was wearing a navy coverall, gloves, and goggles, and had a ventilator mask around his neck. I guessed from his protective gear, compared to Del's usual jeans, Henley, and flannel shirt, that he was the one with arson on his mind.

My fingers tightened around the pepper spray in my jacket pocket, not that it would do a dang bit of good against Tillman's goggles. "Mr. Tillman." My voice only shook a little. "I—"

"I said, who the hell are you?" His voice, unfortunately, shook a lot, which wasn't a great sign. If he was on edge already, I couldn't count on him behaving in a logical manner. As if to confirm that assumption, he kicked the prettily wrapped package aside with a vicious *thwack*, sending it flying all the way into the vestibule. "What are you doing here? This is a closed site."

"The, um, door was open." *Come on, come on.* How long did it take for Bae to move his butt? I'd heard the sirens. My midsection jolted again, and I swallowed hard against impending nausea.

What if the sirens were for something else? What if PJ couldn't get through to 9-1-1? I needed to stall long enough to get Del and me out of here. The problem was that I didn't know whether informing Tillman of imminent police arrival would push him over the edge or make him back down.

There were really far too many potential weapons in this place.

"You're lying. I know I closed it behind me." His gaze darted around as if he'd heard my thought about weapons and was trying to pick out the best one. I just prayed it wouldn't be the pry bar or worse, a lit match. I could dodge a lot of things, but fire wasn't one of them.

"Closed but not locked."

His expression morphed into indignant outrage. "Just because it was unlocked, you're rude enough to waltz right in?"

And really, *that's* what he zeroed in on? Proper entry etiquette? "I was worried about my friend." I glanced down at Del. "Apparently for good reason. Why did—" I bit the inside of my cheek to stop myself from accusing him and possibly setting him off. "Did he have an accident? Construction sites can be so dangerous."

He snorted. "Uh huh. You and I both know he didn't accidentally bash himself on the head."

I noted the two-by-four lying near Del's outstretched arm and winced, but then squared my shoulders. Fine. So he didn't want to play along with my innocent routine. That probably meant he'd already cast me in the role of victim number four. "This isn't the first time you've attacked somebody here, is it?"

His eyes narrowed. "Now I remember you. You're the one who found Jenkins." His scowl deepened, and he took a step toward me. "You found Burns, too. What the hell is wrong with you? Why can't you keep your nose out of my business?"

I probably had a good five inches on Tillman, and at least thirty pounds, but he'd already proven he would kill for his "business," and I was a mechanical engineer, MBA, and ardent crafter holding nothing but a black patent leather clutch and a useless pepper spray. Street combat was *not* one of my skills. I didn't stand a chance against a desperate sociopath.

But I had to try—and I had to trust that PJ would come through for me, like he always did.

On the other hand, if Tillman *was* focused on business, maybe my MBA would be an effective weapon after all. "Mr. Tillman, there is no cost-benefit analysis I've ever seen that proves the ROI on murder is worth the consequences."

He sneered at me and unscrewed the cap on the turpentine can. "That's all you know."

"Then prove it. How could Jenkins's death, Burns's death, Del's—" I fought against a return of that pesky nausea. *Del wasn't dead. And he wouldn't be. Not if I could help it.* "—death possibly be business assets?"

"There's more than one way to cash in on an asset." His calm, matter-of-fact tone was creepier than if he'd gone full Hannibal Lecter. Heck, he sounded more reasonable than Neal. "Especially when it becomes a liability."

I blinked. The hostile building inspector. The snoopy investigative reporter. The disgraced contractor. *The turpentine.* "There's no buyer, is there?"

He lifted an eyebrow, as if acknowledging the hit. "According to all the paperwork there is. And there's no way anyone can trace it back to me." He splashed the turps over a scatter of wood that was far too close to Del's outflung hand for my liking.

"I don't understand. Hank and Margaret would have bought the building. You could have had a real, legal sale without any bloodshed."

"Ah, but if the building is destroyed by a negligent contractor, I get twice the money, or maybe more." He glared at Del. "I should have insisted he post a larger bond. What I'll collect on his is barely worth—"

"Worth his death?" I said hotly, because this guy was really ticking me off. "Worth destroying Margaret and Hank's business?"

He shrugged. "The benefits still outweigh the costs. This is part of a much bigger deal, so I can afford to accept a smaller return on this idiot."

I bristled a bit at that. "He's not an idiot."

"No? Then he should have fixed his damn tool belt so he didn't shed those stupid pliers every time he turned around.

You ask me, this is a win-win. I get the payout and he doesn't get put away for murder."

My belly roiled and the hair at my nape prickled. "Win-*win*?" I gestured at Del's prone form. "Del isn't *winning*. Mr. Jenkins didn't win. Kate didn't win either. And why attack her? Was that only to frame Del? Her death can't have lined your pockets."

A mirthless grin spread across his face. "She was digging too deep. You know what they call her in the real estate development world? The Grim Reaper. And I wasn't about to let her kill this deal."

"So you killed her instead."

He shrugged again. "It's all about maximizing assets and eliminating liabilities. She was a liability. So was that officious jackass Jenkins, who thought he could strong-arm me into cutting him in on the profits." He studied me, his head tilted to one side like a vulture. "And now you're a liability, too. Too bad you didn't just walk on by. Now if you—"

Something flew across the room in a flash of bright paper and trailing ribbon and hit him square in the head. He dropped like a sack of potatoes, landing right in a puddle of turpentine, his expression one of shock.

PJ stalked across the room and enveloped me in a hug. "Are you okay?"

I hugged him back as first responders swarmed the scene. "I'm fine. What did you throw at him?"

"A decorative yet substantial projectile that he very thoughtfully kicked right to me. Isn't it lovely when the villain is dispatched by their own stupid actions?"

I glanced down at Del, who was blinking groggily at the EMTs. "Why did you throw that box if everybody was already here? For that matter, how did you manage to hit him?"

He scrunched up his face. "Weeellll, I expect Detective Hottie will have some words for me, but I couldn't just *wait*. You got the jerkface monologuing, but how long was that likely to last?"

He toed the package, its pretty wrapping significantly worse for wear. "I didn't really mean to hit him. I just wanted to distract him." He grinned at me evilly. "Too bad his inflated ego made his head too big to miss."

CHAPTER TWENTY-TWO

The following day, PJ was waiting for me outside his apartment, practically bouncing on his toes, when I swung by to pick him up.

"You're awfully chipper this morning," I said when he climbed into the car.

He handed me a travel mug, the aroma of my favorite white chocolate peppermint latte making my mouth water. "Who could blame me? My cousin is being released from the hospital with only a tiny concussion, and he's been cleared of all suspicion by Detective Hottie." He took a sip out of his own mug. "Best of all, my BFF doesn't think he's a homicidal maniac." He took another sip. "Although I admit that a good night's sleep and a chai tea latte doesn't hurt."

We were on our way to pick up Del from the hospital. They'd kept him overnight because of the concussion and prolonged exposure to the turpentine fumes but were releasing him today because PJ had sworn up and down that he'd monitor him for any delayed effects for the requisite forty-eight hours.

Technically, the medical requirement was twenty-four hours, but nobody at Jensin Tech needed to know the specifics of a family emergency. I suspected that informing Vinh he was taking two days off had contributed significantly to PJ's mood.

"I hope the action in the Rip Snorter doesn't mean Margaret and Hank can't re-open on Wednesday," I said.

"Nope. In my best oh-so-innocent way, I pumped one of the firefighters—" He shook a finger at me. "Stop giving me that look."

I kept my eyes firmly on the road. "I don't know *what* you're talking about."

"You do so, and that's *my* line. You're imagining naughty things, and I assure you there's no basis for them." He drummed his fingers on his knee. "Unfortunately. I pumped him for *information*, you saucy girl. He said they don't have to secure the scene for very long since they caught the perp." He wiggled happily. "I just *love* saying *perp*."

I shot him a fond sidelong glance. "You're living your *Forensic Files* dreams again."

"Exactly." He wrinkled his nose. "Although I could do without all these random corpses littering our path." He patted my arm. "And may I say that I'm immensely, unutterably, *overwhelmingly* glad that neither you nor Del is among them?"

"You may." I smiled at him. "Because I feel the same. And Peej?" I braked to a stop at the light on the corner of Barnes and Cedar Hills and turned to face him. "I'm really sorry that I suspected Del."

He leaned across the console and kissed my cheek. "You're forgiven. However, I reserve the right to hold this over your head in the future if you ever question my judgment again."

I chuckled, accelerating as traffic began moving through the intersection. "That's fair."

"Good. Oh! My new firefighter bestie told me that since excessive turpentine is considered hazardous, they're sending a hazmat team in to clean it up right away." He grinned. "And charging it to Tillman's insurance."

This time, I full-out laughed. "Somehow, I don't think that's how he imagined his insurance payout would go."

"No." PJ's expression turned stormy. "The big jerkface. I wish I'd hit him harder."

"You hit him hard enough." Del wasn't the only one who'd spent the night in the hospital, although Tillman had apparently been handcuffed to his bed. Bae had been more than a tad miffed with PJ for stepping in, although I got the impression that Bae's ire wasn't just because he couldn't haul Tillman off to jail immediately.

I'd seen the way he'd given PJ an anxious once-over, as though checking to make sure he hadn't sustained any damage.

I pulled into the St. Vincent's Hospital parking garage. "Do we know what was in that package? It certainly packed a punch."

"Not yet." He bit his lip. "Actually, once Del was fully conscious, he was angrier than Detective Hottie for my mad pitching skills. Apparently, the thing belongs to him. But once Detective Hottie assured him that they wouldn't be holding it as evidence, he forgave me for weaponizing it." He slid a sly glance my way as I turned off the car. "Because Tillman was threatening *you*."

"Peej, you need to stop matchmaking. Seriously. Because you are terrible at it."

"Denial does not become you, LaTashia." We both climbed out of the car, and he peered at me over the roof. "I'm convinced I'm brilliant. Just you wait and see."

"Uh huh. Not everybody bonds over felonies like you do."

He stuck his nose in the air and marched toward the pedestrian exit. "I don't know *what* you're talking about."

We walked out of the parking garage and crossed over to the sidewalk that led to the East Pavilion. PJ knew Del's room number, so we walked through the lobby and took the elevator up to the right floor. I waved at the familiar nurse behind the desk—she'd taken one of my card-making classes at Central Paper. PJ just rolled his eyes at her warm greeting.

Perhaps I really did know everybody in this town. Well, I at least knew every serious crafter.

PJ sailed right into Del's room, but I stood back in the doorway. "Delbert!" he crowed. "We've come to spring you from hospital purgatory."

Del was sitting on the side of the bed, his hospital gown straining across his chest and his pale, hairy calves on full display. His eyes widened when he spotted me in the doorway, and he scrabbled the thin white blanket over his lap. "Pete. You didn't have to come."

"Nonsense," PJ declared. "You're my cousin and you've just had a brush with... well, I won't say death because that's just depressing, but with a crazed psycho killer." He wrinkled his nose. "Although I suppose that doesn't sound much better. Besides, you're not allowed to drive yet, and consigning you to a taxi or a ride share?" He flicked his fingers. "I think not."

Del smiled shyly at me. "Hi, Tash. Are you all right? Detective Bae told me you were there." He touched the back of his head where a bandage covered the base of his skull. "I don't remember much about it, to tell you the truth. At least not after Tillman hit me."

I smiled at him. "I'm fine. Are you feeling well enough to go home? I know some people object to the hospital, but you shouldn't check out too soon." It hit me suddenly. Medical insurance! If Del was just starting up his business, his coverage might not be great. "If you can't afford—"

"No, no." He held up both palms, which allowed the blanket to slip. He grabbed it again. "Tillman's liability policy is covering everything. I'm set." He shrugged, further straining the thin gown's fabric. "I don't mind hospitals. The nurses are always great."

One of them—Janine, my crafting friend—bustled in, grinning, a sheaf of papers and a plastic bag that apparently held medication in her hands. "I wish all our patients were as well-behaved as Del. Our jobs would be a snap."

Del smiled at her, warm and friendly. Now why the heck did that send a flash of annoyance zinging through me?

But then Janine winked at me, and her wedding band flashed as she handed the papers to Del. *Right. She's married.* I wanted to kick myself at the wave of relief, and not only because I didn't want to encourage PJ in his matchmaking efforts. I had enough on my plate without adding a possible suitor into the mix.

"I'm not surprised you know Big Del, Tash." She turned to Del and lowered her voice. "Tash knows *everybody.*"

"We just met," I blurted. "Del is PJ's cousin."

"PJ. You're the one Big Del will be staying with, right?"

"That's right." PJ took the bag of medications. "And I'll make sure *Big Del* behaves at home, too."

She chuckled. "You'll have no trouble. He's a teddy bear."

Del blushed, but paid attention to her as she went over the discharge paperwork with him. PJ pulled me aside. "Since clearly the hospital staff have seen him without that dreadful gown, are you interested to know why they're calling him *Big Del?*" he murmured.

Heat rushed up my throat. "Shut up. Do *you* want to talk about your own cousin's... accoutrements?"

He shuddered. "Good point. No."

Janine passed Del a bag containing his clothing. "You can go ahead and get dressed. The doctor has cleared you to be released, so as soon as the orderly arrives with the wheelchair, you're free to go."

Del stood up, clutching his clothing but keeping his back to the wall. "I don't need a wheelchair."

"Hospital policy," Janine said brightly. "No point in fighting it." She patted his arm. "It's been a pleasure. But do us a favor and don't come back, okay?" She jerked her chin at me. "Maybe I'll see you at one of Tash's classes one day instead."

After she left, Del sidled toward the bathroom. "I'll just be a minute."

PJ airily waved a hand. "Take your time, Delbert. Today is all about you." After Del closed the door, PJ wandered over to the window and peered out at the view of the parking garage. "Do you suppose—"

"Ms. Van Buren." Bae's deep voice from the doorway made PJ nearly pirouette. "Mr. Purdy."

I was *very* interested to note that Bae's gaze swept PJ before he cleared his throat and turned to me.

"Detective." PJ, to his credit, kept his voice steady, but he pushed his glasses onto the bridge of his nose with a knuckle, then patted his hair, straightened his shoulders, and stood up a little taller. "Fancy meeting you here."

Bae adjusted the battered box-turned-projectile-weapon nestling in the crook of his arm. "I wanted to catch Mr. Purdy— Mr. Delbert Purdy—before he was released."

"He's getting dressed," I said. "I'm sure he'll be out momentarily."

"Delbert," PJ squawked, "the cops are here for you!"

Del burst out of the bathroom, his shirt only partially buttoned. "What— But they said—"

"Please don't be alarmed," Bae said, studiously not looking at PJ. "I only wanted to give you this." He set the rather battered package on the bedside table. "We don't need it any longer. I also wanted to let you know that we're transferring Mr. Tillman to the county jail now." He gave Del the half smile that usually sent PJ's blood pressure skyrocketing, although it didn't seem to have that effect on Del. "As a part of the plea deal his lawyer is recommending, he's given a full confession."

"Deals seem to be his thing," I said dryly.

Bae inclined his head. "Indeed. He's admitted that burning the building had been his plan for months, from before he hired Mr. Purdy. In fact, he explicitly hired Mr. Purdy because Kate Burns's articles led him to believe Mr. Purdy was either incompetent, corrupt, or both." He focused his intense gaze on Del. "Imagine his dismay when he discovered you were neither."

PJ sidled over to me and murmured out of the side of his mouth, "Did Detective Hottie make a joke?"

Bae glanced over at us, one eyebrow cocked. "Merely an observable truth."

"Just shoot me now," PJ muttered, then blinked. "I mean, obviously that's just a euphemism. Or a metaphor. Or a hyperbole. Or something, because I would never tell somebody who actually *carries a gun* to shoot me, because that would be ludicrous."

"Peej," I said gently. "Maybe it would be a good idea to stop talking?"

"Right," he said, voice strangled. "Stopping now."

"What about Mr. Jenkins?" Del asked.

"Originally, Jenkins was in on the scam. However, he started to get cold feet and threatened to report Tillman to the authorities. Tillman bribed him for a while, but apparently decided to cut his losses. He left the body at the construction site to raise suspicion about Mr. Purdy. He needed the money for a new real estate development deal and his partners were pressing him for his share of the funds."

"How did Kate Burns find out about it?" I asked.

"She was originally investigating the Hillsboro Promenade scam, when two historically protected buildings somehow burned to the ground because of suspicious electrical fires. So she was already in the area. When Tillman hired Mr. Purdy, her obsession with her brother's death made her change her focus."

I cut a sidelong glance at Del. "Did she know about Tillman's arson plans?"

"I don't believe so. But he was afraid she'd get closer, or else interfere with his intent to frame Mr. Purdy."

Del ran his hand over his face. "I knew I should have checked Tillman's credentials. Just because he drives a '66 GTO like me doesn't make him a stand-up guy."

"If the plea deal falls through, we may need your testimony, so if you wouldn't mind letting us know your whereabouts…"

"Don't worry," Del said, his gaze flickering to PJ and me. "I'm not going anywhere."

Bae turned to me, his mouth tilted in a smile, and PJ all but whimpered beside me. "Ms. Van Buren, we'll need your statement, too."

"Of course. I'm happy to help in any way I can."

Bae nodded to each of us—PJ last—and left as silently as he'd arrived.

PJ sagged against the wall. "Honestly. If he weren't so infuriating, he'd be my perfect man."

The orderly arrived and Del settled into the wheelchair, the package in his lap. He kept up a relatively cheerful conversation with Del on the way to the elevator.

"Excuse me," I said. "I'll go get the car and bring it around to the entrance."

I raced on ahead of them. Just as I'd climbed into my car and started the ignition, my cell phone started playing Fleetwood Mac's *Gypsy*, Margaret's ringtone. The call routed through the CR-V's Bluetooth system. "Margaret? Is everything okay?" I'd only spoken to her briefly after the incident with Tillman yesterday.

"More than okay!" The excitement in her voice was clearly audible, even under several tons of concrete parking structure. "Tillman's accepted our offer on the building!"

"That's fabulous!" I pulled out of my spot and headed for the hospital entrance. "What changed his mind?"

Her chuckle burred over the line. "Let's just say he was a motivated seller. Apparently, he's about to incur some significant legal fees and wanted to get this settled before the court froze his assets for damages to his victims."

"Congratulations! I'm sorry it fell out the way it did, but I'm glad the whole thing has a bit of a silver lining."

"We're starting renovation plans already, and I fully expect you to help me with the decor."

"Absolutely. Especially if Hank lets me sample any signature cocktails he comes up with."

"You know he will, although probably not while we're working on the designs. Those things are potent. Um..." Her tone turned diffident. "Do you suppose you could put in a good word with PJ's cousin?"

I eased the CR-V to the curb, where PJ and Del waited with the orderly. "For what? And why not ask PJ to put in the good word? He *is* Del's cousin."

"Yes, but you're Del's crush."

"Margaret—"

"Don't be coy, Tash. It's not a good look on you. We'd like to hire Del to be our GC, but given his experience, he may have developed an aversion to the building."

"If you hold on for a minute, I'll ask him. PJ and I are collecting him from the hospital as we speak."

She squawked about something, but her words were drowned by the bustle of PJ and Del arguing over who would sit in the back versus who'd ride shotgun. I'm not entirely sure who technically won, but PJ ended up next to me. He spotted Margaret's name on the dashboard console.

"You're talking to Margaret? Hello, Margaret, my love!"

"Margaret and Hank are buying the building," I said, and PJ whooped. "They'd also like to know..." I met Del's gaze in the rearview mirror. "...if you'd consider being their GC."

Del blinked. "They want me? Even after what happened?"

"Especially after what happened," Margaret said. "But not if you'd rather avoid a place that has such unfortunate memories."

He held my gaze, his cheeks pinking with his blush. "Not all the memories are unfortunate. I'd be honored."

"Excellent," she said. "Now get over here for some celebratory scones."

I turned to face Del. "Is that okay? Do you feel up to it?" When he nodded, I said, "You're on, Margaret. Tell Hank to fire up the teapots. We're over at St. Vincent, so we won't be long."

CHAPTER TWENTY-THREE

PJ kept up a steady chatter about Portland sightseeing, *Forensic Files*, and Mary Pickford's latest cat toy, with random tangents involving Bae's butt in his navy-blue detective suit and complaints about Vinh and the merger. Del didn't say much, but whenever I checked in the rearview, he was smiling softly, and his gaze was on me even though he didn't meet my eyes again.

I parked behind the tearoom, but before I could open my door, Del cleared his throat. "Tash?" PJ and I both turned in our seats. Del held up the package in its tattered wrapping. "I'm not sure what state this is in, but before PJ decided to use it as a catapult, it was for you."

My heart fluttered a bit, not gonna lie. "Me?"

He nodded. "You've done so much for Pete—"

"Delbert," PJ warned, but Del ignored him.

"And you made me feel welcome, too. Now I owe you even more. You didn't just save my behind. You saved my life." He held it out. "If you don't like it, if it was damaged, or if it's not enough, I—"

PJ snatched the package. "No take-backsies, Delbert, and stop being so *abject*. That's also not macho." He plopped the box in my lap—although it was big enough that it honked the horn. "Whoops. Just open it, LaTashia."

I could no more ignore Del's heartfelt words than I could withstand PJ's drill sergeant orders, so I peeled away the tattered wrapping paper. Underneath was a double layer of corrugated cardboard, and inside that... "Oh, Del," I breathed. "This is gorgeous."

It was a puzzle box similar to the picture PJ had shown me when he was encouraging me to submit my art to that craft magazine, except this one was even more exquisite. Beautiful, with mitered joints, three different kinds of wood, and a finish that gleamed even behind the CR-V's tinted windows.

"I was able to finish it more quickly than I thought, since work on Tillman's project got delayed."

So that's where he'd been when he hadn't been at the site. My face heated, guilt burning in my throat. While I'd been suspecting Del of planning and executing murders, he'd been building this magnificent box. For me.

"Thank you," I managed to choke out. "I'm not sure I deserve something this lovely."

"You do," Del said softly. "You definitely do."

"Darn right, she does." PJ took the box from me and set it on the console. "She's a goddess, just like I've always said. But right now, she's a goddess who's delaying our tea and scones. You can moon over the box later, LaTashia. For right now—"

My cell phone pinged with a text, but since the box was in the way, PJ picked up the phone, glancing at it reflexively. "Um..."

"It's not from Neal, is it? Downsizing me?"

"As if." But PJ sighed and bit his lip.

I wasn't sure I could take another shock. "What is it?"

"I'm so sorry, Tash. It's from Rhonda. You didn't get the house."

My stomach hollowed as I slumped in my seat. "I didn't?"

"Apparently, the owners accepted a much higher bid, one outside your budget. I'm so sorry." PJ gently rubbed my arm as I fought back tears of disappointment. "But what about that Craftsman bungalow we saw?"

"The one in Hillsboro? With the orange shag carpet?"

PJ rolled his eyes, but didn't stop the soothing pats. "Don't get sidetracked by appearances. Especially since appearances can be so fleeting. The house itself was hella cute from outside. It has great bones, and location, location, location. The neighborhood is way better than the other one and downtown Hillsboro is within walking distance. I'm seeing cocktails at Pembroke's in our future."

"But it needs so much work," I wailed.

"And the other one didn't? Just think of it as one big craft project." He stopped patting my arm and poked it instead. "How can you resist?"

"And don't worry," Del said with a smile that warmed my insides. "No matter how much work it needs, you've got yourself a contractor."

A Message from
Nelle & C.K.

Dear Reader,

Thank you so much for reading *Mixed Media*, our second Crafty Sleuth cozy mystery. More shenanigans will follow, but if you missed Tash and PJ's first adventure, be sure to check it out in *Die Cut*.

If you have time, we'd be so grateful if you could leave a review on Amazon, Goodreads, or other review sites. Reviews and word-of-mouth are more important than you can imagine to independent authors like us.

Active on Facebook? Then we'd love for you to join us in our Crafty Sleuth reader group!

All our best,
—Nelle & C.K.

Also by
Nelle Heran

With C.K. Eastland

Crafty Sleuth Mysteries
Die Cut
Mixed Media
Found Objects (coming soon)

Writing as E.J. Russell

Find E.J. on Audible at https://ejr.pub/ejr-audible

M/M Paranormal Romance and Mysteries
Mythmatched Universe
Quest Investigations Mysteries (*Five Dead Herrings, The Hound of
the Burgervilles, The Lady Under the Lake, Death on Denial*)
Fae Out of Water Trilogy (*Cutie and the Beast, The Druid Next
Door, Bad Boy's Bard*)
Supernatural Selection Trilogy (*Single White Incubus, Vampire
With Benefits, Demon on the Down-Low*)
Other Mythmatched *Romances (Howling on Hold, Witch Under
Wraps, The Skinny on Djinni*)
Possession in Session (free with newsletter signup)
Cursed is the Worst (free with YBBB promotion in 2022)

Enchanted Occasions (*Best Beast, Nudging Fate, Devouring Flame*)

Royal Powers (*Duking It Out, Duke the Hall, King's Ex*)

Other Stand-Alone (*Purgatory Playhouse, Monster Till Midnight*)

M/M Supernatural Suspense
Art Medium (*The Artist's Touch, Tested in Fire*, Omnibus edition)
Legend Tripping (*Stumptown Spirits, Wolf's Clothing*)

M/M Historical Romance (*Silent Sin*)

M/M Contemporary Romance (*The Thomas Flair, Mystic Man, Clickbait, For a Good Time, Call…*)

M/M Contemporary Holiday Shorts (*The Probability of Mistletoe, An Everyday Hero, A Swants Soiree, Christmas Kisses*)

M/F Contemporary Romance *The Boyfriend Algorithm*

Also by
C.K. Eastland

With Nelle Heran

Crafty Sleuth Mysteries
Die Cut
Mixed Media
Found Objects (coming soon)

Writing as C. Morgan Kennedy

Haven, Oregon Series
A Coffee-Driven Life (coming soon)
A Forgotten Life (coming soon)

About The
Authors

Nelle Heran (she/her) has always loved mysteries. She cut her teeth on Nancy Drew before graduating to Agatha Christie, Dorothy L. Sayers, Josephine Tey, and Charlotte MacLeod. Full disclosure: She stopped watching *Murder, She Wrote* when she began identifying the murderer before the opening credits finished rolling.

Nelle also writes LGBTQ romance and mystery as E.J. Russell (https://ejrussell.com). She lives in rural Oregon with her Curmudgeonly Husband, enjoys visits from her wonderful adult children, and indulges in good books, red wine, and the occasional hyperbole.

Find out more about Nelle, including social media links, at her website, https://nelleheran.com.

C.K. Eastland (she/her) fell in love with mysteries when she first discovered reruns of the original Hanna-Barbera series *Scooby-Doo, Where Are You?* Over time, she graduated to Sherlock Holmes and is currently addicted to *Midsomer Murders*.

C.K. also writes contemporary swirl romance mysteries as C. Morgan Kennedy (https://cmorgankennedy.com). Recently she moved from Portland, Oregon, to Chicagoland for her day job. Still nesting in her new condo, C.K. spends her mornings and weekends researching famous Victorian homes, scrapbooking, and watching way too many Star Wars fandom reviews on YouTube.

Find out more about C.K., including social media links, at her website, https://ckeastland.com.

Acknowledgements

We owe a debt to so many for help and support on this book! Massive thanks go out to our fabulous editors, Shéa MacLeod and Meg DesCamp; to Markayla Blake of Covers in Color for giving us the covers of our dreams; to our wonderful beta readers—lyric apted, Lisa Leoni-Kinley, and Kenya Goree-Bell; to Maggie, owner of The Clockwork Rose Tea Emporium in downtown Beaverton, OR, and her husband Harold, who gave us a welcoming place to sip tea and laugh till our sides hurt—and for providing the inspiration for The Airship Ambassador Tearoom and Apothecary and its lovely owners!

From C.K.:
Crazy love and thanks to my personal cheerleaders Jessie Smith, Linda Mercury and her Charming Man, Kenya Goree-Bell, Pamala Knight, and the Retreat Beach Babes (my scrapbooking circle): Jen, Jan, Donna Lyn, Kim, Karen, and Anne. Nelle—you are an amazing partner in fictional crime.

From Nelle:
Love and appreciation to C.K. for being the inspiration for the Crafty Sleuth series (because she basically *is* Tash), and to my family—Jim, Hana, Nick, Ross, and Billy—for endless support.

And of course, from both of us, thanks to you, our readers, for accompanying us on this journey! Because of you, we can continue to do what we love!